C0-AUQ-353

THERE WERE
TWO
PIRATES

A COMEDY OF DIVISION

"Did ever pirate roll
His soul in guilty dreaming,
And wake to find that soul
With peace and virtue beaming?"

THERE WERE
TWO
PIRATES

A COMEDY OF DIVISION

by
JAMES BRANCH CABELL

Decorations by
John O'Hara Cosgrave II

FARRAR, STRAUS AND COMPANY, INC.
NEW YORK
1946

FOR MARJORIE KINNAN RAWLINGS

Who more than any other person has given fame to the old ways of Florida; whose actual home is beyond the City Gates; and whom I am proud to rank as a friend.

CONTENTS

EDITORIAL NOTE

I F EVER YOU HAVE PASSED a winter in Florida, attentive to its legends, but above all if you have visited Tampa, where since 1904 the renown of José Gasparilla has been honored almost every year with a befitting ceremonial reverence, then a part of the story here narrated will be familiar to you; but not much of it. Were there nothing else, no man can write out his autobiography with the precise and serene detachment of an historian, who knows so little about what really did happen that he hardly ever needs to bother about facts.

That José Gasparilla at his decease had left, in addition to his now perished diary for the years 1784–1791, an autobiography likewise, has always been the hope of many students of Florida's history. There seemed to be no occasion, however, for research workers to pursue this autobiography in St. Augustine, inasmuch as with that city, so far as went any published historical records, or even any legend, Gasparilla had no alliance. His supposed theatre, ashore, had been limited to the West Coast of Florida.

Meanwhile, it is easy to imagine that in St. Augustine the descendants of his wife, as the possessors of the hunted-for manuscript, were not at all eager to make public the remarkable document which had been left by their revered step-grandfather; and with their attitude one, upon the whole, sympathizes. It is possible to admire the adamantean morality of Gasparilla's high-mindedness without being quick to advertise his inclusion in one's home circle.

Time, at long last, has dispelled this embarrassment. To-day the José Gasparilla who died, not as history puts it, in Charlotte Harbor in the December of 1821, but during the first week of the July of 1828 in St. Augustine, has become a family connection so comfortably remote that the fourteen surviving descendants of his stepchildren are well enough willing, for history's correction, to allow his true story to be published—or at any rate, the story which he declared to be true. So hereinafter you may find it, with various excisions such as, for one reason or another, have appeared necessary.

—For as a writer, it must be admitted, José Gasparilla possessed no talent for selecting the essential. It is not merely that, when mid-course in narrative, he will pause to deliberate whether a particular event happened upon the thirtieth or the thirty-first of the month, or to recall the Christian name of the slave-trader's widow who made his flag, or to verify the precise date of the accession of King Charles the Fourth, when not any one of these circumstances is important to the story in hand. An uncommonly literal-minded person, you feel forgivingly, is here striving to be wholly accurate; so that even when a detail or two may have slipped his memory, he must needs be halting, yet again, to record his forgetfulness, or his conceded uncertainty, as to this or the other trifle. "To the best of my recollection, he was a

viii

native of Santander," he remarks, for example, concerning Captain Ruiz. Such caution, howsoever far from being a literary grace note, may be hailed as praiseworthy when you regard it as a moral obligation.

The trouble is that Gasparilla's painstaking, in the complete manuscript version of his autobiography, goes very far farther; and becomes unendurable. For one matter, the man catalogued (not quite Homerically) almost all the ships with which he had dealt in the course of his profession; he put down the sum total collected from each; he stated from what port the vessel had sailed, as well as her destination; and he then added, whenever this was possible, a memorandum as to the ship's owner and her captain. His thoroughness, irrespective of its contribution to Gasparilla's success in life, does not make for enjoyable reading; and so, has been curtailed.

He has included likewise the abnormal tragedy of Father Verdago and the two choir boys—whose story is, in itself, both interesting and sedately shocking, but has no particular bearing upon the story of Gasparilla, which it serves merely to interrupt. He yet furthermore has set forth, at considerable length, an account of the unfortunate love affair of his lieutenant, Roderigo Lopez, in Avilés, and the three murders which it entailed; yet this also has not anything to do with the story of Gasparilla, beyond accounting for the part which Lopez played in the mutiny. And at least a half dozen similar instances (including a regrettably indelicate ten-page conversation with Teresa Antonia as to her mother's amours) might here be cited but for the fear of making this brief preface sound as prolix as one has found the manuscript with which it deals.

All such excrescences one has tried to remove; or rather, one has tried to extricate from a large welter of irrelevances the strange story of José Gasparilla, not as history, but as he himself, narrates it.

St. Augustine, Florida
14 April 1946

PART ONE

"What lad, when skies were bluer,
And hardihood stayed whole,
Hath found that aught seemed truer
Than that a loyal soul
Must loyally pursue her
Whose winning seemed life's goal?"

I

BEING NOT UNAWARE of that interest with which the run of humankind regard the doings of pre-eminent persons, I, José Gasparilla, record here that my first important achievement was performed at Montserrat, in the Spanish province of Barcelona, upon the feast day of the Holy Innocents, in the year of our Lord 1756; for there and then I was born.

At the age of eighteen I entered the Naval Academy. I became in due course a lieutenant; and serving under Captain Pedro Olmos y de Sanibel—an hidalgo whose deportment and ancestry, as I recall with affection, were but a little inferior to my own—I, during this bright period of my youth's innocence, took part in four years of rapine and butchery, in obedience to the usual demands of patriotism, until after the Treaty of Versailles had been agreed upon.

By this compact, it may be recalled, the usurped province of Florida was yielded up by the thieving English

3

and restored to Spain. I had private and urgent reasons (to which I shall recur in the sequel) for going into Florida without delay; and so, with the assistance of my fellow lieutenant, Roderigo Lopez, and of our chaplain, Father Martin León Verdago, of Seville, a mutiny was arranged upon the festival of the Conversion of St. Paul, whose intercession for our success I duly invoked upon the eve of this momentous occasion.

Thirty-eight out of the ship's crew of sixty joined in with the three of us to dispatch the other officers and the seamen who remained loyal to sentiments such as I, for one, admired as relics of a more highly impassioned era, but for the sake of my own welfare was compelled to discourage. To the last words of our deposed captain, in particular, I listened with reverence; they were biassed by disapproval; they bordered even upon the denunciatory; and yet, so complete was my affection for the indomitable old gentleman that I blew out his brains in a warm glow of admiration.

When the last corpse had been thrown overboard, I in this manner found myself, now newly turned twenty-seven, to have become the sole owner of the *Floridablanca*, a trim sloop of war armed with eight guns; and I sailed westward, to ignite that glory which, like a balefire, glitters about the unparalleled fame of Gasparilla.

2

I DID NOT LEAVE SPAIN, you may depend upon it, without devoting a candle to St. Eulalia, in the great cathedral of Barcelona (I mean the city of that name) and indulging in the dear miseries of a temporary leave-taking from Isabel de Castro.

When I had told my life's one love of how I was now embarked toward opulence, as the proprietor of my own ship, she spoke with tender reproach.

"I cannot but wonder at you, José; for it is not suitable that a gentleman of Spain should be going into trade. Your ancestors are no doubt astir with indignation in every one of their tombs."

"I admit, my dearest," I replied, "that this possibility has troubled me. Yet my ancestors ought to consider that it was they, precisely, who made of me a penniless orphan. By every rule of good breeding and philanthropy, the doings of a penniless orphan are regarded with charity; and his endeavors to become self-supporting should be counted as praiseworthy."

"Nevertheless, José, the police are not always broad-minded—"

"Furthermore, my adored Isabel, my proposed venture, should Heaven consider my prayers with indulgence, will not be limited to mercantile desk-work. I intend, rather, to become a king with a statesmanlike interest in commerce. And for anyone to find himself the progenitor of a reigning monarch must be, to even the most exigent of my ancestors, a source of pride."

"Nor am I sure, José, that it is right of you to be making off with the King of Spain's ship, now that his health is getting to be what everybody says it is, and after you had promised to him fidelity."

"You forget, Isabel, that I too am a king in bud; and it is the custom of all kings to discard fidelity in our dealings with one another."

"That is logic, perhaps. But ah, my dearest, no innocent young girl can display logic in all situations. And that reminds me, now that you have killed so many persons in their beds, and even your own god-father—"

"My pet, but you speak with an ignorance of nautical affairs which is not suitable to a sea captain's betrothed wife. They for the most part were in their bunks or their hammocks, whereas Captain Sanibel and some fifteen others of them died fighting and after having indulged in regrettably profane language."

6

"Even so, José, and while of course no well-brought-up young woman would dream of defending profanity, still it must have been most upsetting, so far as they felt about it; and it is their feelings we ought to consider—"

"The sentiment is characteristic of your sweet and compassionate nature, Isabel; but a penniless orphan has to consider first his own needs."

"—And my feelings too, José, because the thought that I should have been more or less the cause of it all has upset me too; so that I really cannot take a bright view of your leaving me and perhaps finding some other girl that you like better over in that only half-civilized America. I mean one of those red Indian women with nothing on her whatever except a piece of Spanish moss, like the pictures in a geography, because everybody knows what you sailors are."

"You speak at random, my adored one; for to you my heart will remain faithful forever. And so, because of my love for you, I have entered the only course which offered—to a penniless orphan—any chance to acquire that modest competence without which we may not hope to live in comfort. Moreover, it appeared my plain duty to consider our children's welfare."

"But how do you know, José, that we shall have any children, and especially now that they will be trying to hang you for stealing your ship?"

"The habit is common to both of our families, you must remember. I do not allude to ship-stealing. I mean that our parents and our grandparents alike had children; and that every known law of heredity thus forces me to believe we shall emulate them."

"Yes, that is true, José, when one comes to think about it, and does not worry about your killing people, over and above your regular duties as a lieutenant in the Navy. So far as I can see, and except for the police, it comes to pretty much the same thing. But then, to the other side—"

"There can be no other side, heart's darling. To the need of our children for daily food and a sound education I dared not remain obdurate. Such callousness would have been unworthy of José Gasparilla. It has followed, from these tender considerations, that in no long time I intend to amass 500,000 pesos; the sum is not enormous; but as I calculate the requirements of our probable home circle, it will suffice. I shall then return to you; and the felicity of our future, as well as of our own dear offspring, will be unmitigated."

With that settled, we embraced yet again; and so parted.

And I have been at no small pains, do you let me assure you, to record this conversation with my heart's fond idol without any untoward interruption or commentary by myself, so that my readers might acquire the tenor of it unperturbedly; and might not be bewildered, as I was, by the bright personal beauty of Isabel de Castro all during the while when we thus talked together, in the front parlor of her revered parents' home, upon either the thirtieth or the thirty-

8

first day of January 1784. I think it was the latter. I appear to have made no memorandum.

—For I desire in this way to impress upon my readers the circumstance that my adored Isabel not infrequently veiled the most noble sentiments with a striking simplicity of intelligence; and thus added to the excellence of her character a yet further pre-eminence.

Even so, in the bewitching presence of her unspeakable and unmatched physical charms, you, my discerning reader (whom hereabouts I am presupposing to be of the male sex), would have inclined, one grants you, to overlook this particular vocal virtue. You would have noted, rather, that its displayer was young and graceful and wholly lovely, to a degree beyond any describing by even the more liberally endowed poets who, at various periods, have contributed to the world's best literature. You would have observed, in short, that without having any formal warrant issued by grave reason and countersigned by austere reflection, you loved, and must love forever (with a pallid imitating of my own gigantic affection), the beautiful small goddess from whom I was now departing, temporarily.

3

THE WESTWARD VOYAGE of my expedition proved uneventful. When during the first week of April (upon the feast day of St. Mary the Egyptian) we sighted the coast of Florida, we followed the long line of tiny islets which extends from Biscayne Bay to Key West. We thus entered the Gulf of Mexico and turned north. We came by-and-by to an excellent harbor, upon the West Coast of Florida, protected by five islands, all which proved to be uninhabited.

"Behold your kingdom," said Father Verdago.

"In fact," said Lopez, "one may live here in fair comfort."

"It is not comfort for which we are seeking"—so did I rebuke him—"but activities of a more lofty cast."

I then requested my crew to dispose themselves upon the warm sands, and for their benefit I summarized my intentions.

"Gentlemen," I remarked, to my sturdy ruffians,

with a tactful flavor of exaggeration, "we have reached our goal. You behold the stage upon which all of us may hope henceforward to figure as heroes, now that in this harbor we abandon the ungracious rôle of mutineers and become magnates of commerce."

Cries of applause here interrupted me, interspersed with not a few murmurs of surprise.

"Upon these islands," I explained, "will be that which is termed technically, by naval strategists, the base of our operations. The location is eligible. To the west and south of us pass merchant vessels with varied cargoes. It will be our employment to lighten these cargoes of their more valuable items. During the pursuit of this enterprise, the need may arise, now and then, for us to destroy human life. It is a task in which, I may say without boasting, we are all proficient. As members of the Spanish Navy, gentlemen, you have performed this task repeatedly in defence of your native land and for the glory of your former monarch, King Charles the Third.

"The allegiance which you paid to him," I resumed affably, "you will now transfer to me. That is all which gratitude demands of you, gentlemen, at this instant. You will find in Gasparilla, the King of Pirates, an enlightened and kindly chief executive. Yet furthermore, as my first formal act in office, I herewith declare war against all other existent governments; so that by every one of you these oncoming homicides may be attended to with an unstained conscience, as being patriotic necessities directed against the enemies of our way of living.

"Nor, gentlemen," I continued, after the subsiding of their cheers, "is it only to your more noble emotions that I address myself; for I admit that human nature is appreciably removed from being immaculate. No one of us is entirely unselfish. We who shall be revered henceforward as overlords of the Gulf of Mexico, and of the Spanish Main, and perhaps of the Seven Seas in general, are about to become world-famous heroes; but it is not in this impressive attitude that we shall need to face twenty-four hours of every day. —For the hero has his human side, nay, even his foibles. He does not scorn relaxation; he is not of necessity a spoilsport," I pointed out; and I smiled indulgently.

"It is for this reason, gentlemen, I now assure you that, between our valiant crusades against the sordid efforts of our enemies to accumulate crude wealth through the ignoble avenues of commerce, we shall find ample opportunities to appraise life's lighter and more dulcet aspects. We shall take many captives. We shall become opulent beyond the dreams of Crœsus—nay, even after that monarch had arisen from a prolonged banquet of an unusually indigestible nature. All such of our captives as are fine-looking women we shall treat with mercy; and in their beds we shall be repaid for the exercise of this virtue."

My hearers chuckled at this point in my address; and it is to be feared their thoughts became unchaste. I explained, therefore, that I referred to the lawful delights of matrimony alone, for which Father Verdago would be at hand to qualify all applicants; and I resumed my discourse.

"Furthermore, gentlemen, I forewarn you that so soon as the condition of our treasury may warrant the liquidating of my endeavors with a fair profit, I shall retire from the exacting duties of your commander in chief into the private but praiseworthy amenities of begetting a half-dozen or so young Gasparillas, with the assistance of that paragon among earth's women to whom my faith is pledged forever. You will, it stays possible, lament my departure; but you will lament in vain. For the present, let us dismiss your bereavement."

I then added, in a mood somewhat less emotional,—

"It suffices, gentlemen, that to-day I can offer to you adventure and opulence, upon the sole condition that you tender to Gasparilla, the King of Pirates, an oath of unswerving fidelity."

Applause answered me yet again; and the rogues hastened forward to kneel and to kiss my hand. It was a proud moment. Modesty alone prevents me from admitting that it was an historic moment pregnant with very many happenings such as yet stagger the imagination of any person who speaks, or who endeavors to write plausibly, about José Gasparilla.

PART TWO

"When love assumes the guiding
Of blood-stained buccaneers,
And yet remains abiding
For more than seven years,
How tactless any chiding
Of piracy appears!"

4

THAT PROVIDENCE SMILED upon my vigor and industry, and it may be upon a few spurts of genius also, the world knows. Our islands I duly christened, as Sanibel (in memory of our deceased commander), and Cayo Costa, and Pine Island, and Captiva; but the northernmost of them I named Gasparilla Island, in honor, not of myself, whose nature has always been deficient in personal vanity to a signal degree, but of my knightly and renowned ancestors. Upon each island, excepting only Captiva, we builded houses of palmetto logs, which we thatched with palm leaves.

When our homes had been thus established and put in order, and the needed privies erected, we set forth upon the *Gasparilla* (as my sloop had been re-named by popular acclamation), and off the north coast of Cuba we took our first prize, in the form of a merchant ship, the *Concepçion*, of Bilbao, and owned by the Cerda

Brothers, then on her way from Palos to Havana. She was captured without trouble; and after I had addressed the surviving members of her crew with such eloquence as I could muster, eleven of them elected to join my forces. The others were killed and thrown overboard.

Upon this brig we found a couple of women, whom seven of my men offered to mislead from the path of virtue; I ordered these hard-set bachelors to draw straws for the wenches; and for the benefit of the two winners, Father Verdago at once performed the sacrament of matrimony, in which I took part by giving away both of the brides. We selected from the ship's cargo and furnishings those articles which I thought needful, and we then sank the vessel.

Such was my modest beginning as a buccaneer; and inasmuch as the daily round of any and all professional labors must necessarily tend toward repetitiousness, I shall not trouble the reader with many details of my advancement in prosperity. One sea-fight is much like another, nor did I find any special variety in the routine work of dealing with our male prisoners after the conclusion of hostilities. During these final passages, we for economy's sake employed cutlasses, because our supply of gunpowder was limited.

I record merely that the secret of my success, or rather, its self-evident cause, was my application to piracy of the discipline which I had learned to honor in the Spanish Navy, under my beloved commander and esteemed friend, Captain Pedro de Sanibel. Only

too many of the buccaneer captains who preceded me
in the Western Hemisphere had been persons of flighty
and irreligious habits such as in the long run could not
but lead to unreverent criticism, or even to a similar
disrespect for decency and order, among their subor-
dinates. I avoided this error. In dealing with my followers I maintained the dignity which befits a chief
executive, in the same instant that among them I fos-
tered thrift and piety and subservience and yet other
desirable traits of sound citizenship.

In this manner we were enabled, throughout our
business ventures upon the high seas, to kill, and to steal,
and to demolish, without any depressing compunctions,
because I had made it clear to my men that we performed these duties in an heroic defence of our new
homeland and of the Gasparillan way of living; but
ashore we obeyed the laws of my kingdom, which dis-
couraged any large excess of unfair dealing, or of
vituperation, or of imbecility seasoned with moral
fervor, or of any unhumanly high standards in talk,
along with a great many other necessaries of the patriot
when his hearthstone has become imperilled in the
windy chaos he calls his mind.

5

INASMUCH AS I HAVE but very rarely enjoyed killing my fellow creatures, it followed that as my reputation increased in magnificence, I took measures to abate a vast deal of economic wastefulness, through the introduction of more enlightened methods into the conduct of my profession. The name of Gasparilla had become extremely terrible; and this fact I now utilized, in a shared service of altruism and of thrift, after the looting and destruction of twelve merchant vessels had conferred upon me fame.

I discarded the conventional flag adorned with a skull and crossbones, which had become common to all pirates. I designed for my sloop a more handsome ensign. This trade-mark, if I may so call it, was constructed under my directions at Fernandina, by a widow in reduced circumstances, whose name was either Mariana or Maria Manucy. I am not certain as to her Christian name; but her former husband had been a ship's captain in the slave trade, and her needle work was far more than satisfactory. This ensign displayed upon a black field a human skeleton, worked in silver threads, holding up an hour glass half-filled with blood, so that my clients could know, well in advance, that they had to deal with no petty sea-thief but with Gasparilla.

I fired a shot across the bow of their vessel. If they showed fight, I responded in kind. I boarded the ship, and I destroyed all whom I found there, without upon these regrettable occasions feeling myself at liberty to show mercy toward anybody. I instead pointed the moral lesson which I felt it was my duty to convey by slitting all throats impartially with my own case knife. This labor, howsoever tedious, was acknowledged by everyone to lend to my work an unique touch of distinction.

But when common-sense prevailed, and the ship surrendered, then I exhibited the magnanimity of a Christian gentleman. I went aboard quietly; I took charge of one half the money I discovered, dividing it fairly with its previous owners. I selected with a sparing hand such other valuables as we needed, including the women whom my men fancied, and I permitted my followers to indulge in no violence or rude language. The ship was then allowed to go about her own business unmolested.

Now my predecessors and my fellow practitioners did not show any such tact or consideration for those whom truth compels me to describe as being not so much their clients as their victims. In the revolting rôle of mere avaricious bunglers, they attacked without parley; when their crude methods were gorged with that which reflection cannot but label an undeserved success, they murdered and they plundered without discrimination; and they concluded their unpraiseworthy behavior by destroying the ship also, so as to leave not any physical traces, or a living witness, of their boorishness.

It is no wonder that, with the world's oceans infected by such ruffians, Gasparilla attained to that unique glory which now attended his name even when it was whispered in terror. —For the King of Pirates, it was known, dealt otherwise: you had merely to respect the wishes of Gasparilla in order to avoid theft and manslaughter; and so, even if I cannot assert that I became ardently popular among merchant captains and their passengers, yet inasmuch as my clients found it a minor disaster to pay toll to me, in the not immoderate form of fifty per cent of their moneys, and of an occasional wife or daughter, rather than to combine the inconvenience of being left penniless with the calamity of a slit throat, it followed that my abstentions from any irregular wrongdoing did, in the long run, produce handsome dividends.

6

My crew at this period averaged eight officers and about fifty able-bodied seamen. Such men as I had the misfortune to lose in battle or through accident were replaced constantly by the more eligible volunteers from captured vessels, who, after I addressed them, evinced almost always a flattering desire to enter my service rather than to become sharks' food.

We took only such women captives as we needed either for matrimonial purposes or housework, sparing all those who were too age-stricken or feeble to be of any use to us; and if it was the personal appearance of these female prisoners rather than their innate virtues which determined their future upon my five islands, such is the common fate of the gentle sex in all portions of the world.

The elderly or the ugly I assigned to duty as our chambermaids, our laundresses, and our cooks. For the more comely, such of my men as wanted her drew lots, and the winner was married to the young woman by Father Verdago, who now ranked as the King of Pirates' private chaplain.

But I of course remained unmarried; I was well-nigh the sole celibate in my island kingdom: for should the reader imagine that at any instant during the prime of Gasparilla's perhaps unsurpassed glory my heart was inclined to deviate, by one hair's breadth, from its complete loyalty to Isabel de Castro, he would miscomprehend the nature of true love.

To the other side, there is no profession but has its traditionary time-hallowed code; and of a pirate captain in successful practice, as I noted with dismay, an inordinate rapacity for women was expected by even his most lenient critics.

For me to have neglected this convention would not merely have led to the general public's disappointment; it would have invited a suspicion that I, after all, was not utterly relentless; and the commercial value of my celebrity would very soon have become diminished by insidious rumors that, in private, great Gasparilla now and then gave heed to the counsels of virtue. People, in brief, would have grown less afraid of me; and this awkward mischance I could not afford, now that I followed a profession in which my chief asset was the terror which I inspired.

Through the dictates of prudence, I was thus led to violate the better-looking of our female captives; and to maintain in my home upon Gasparilla Island a succession of mistresses, whom after a short period of dalliance I married off to one or another of my followers.

But at all times my heart remained faithful to Isabel.

7

DURING THE FOURTH AUTUMN of such professional labors as have been recorded, I was so fortunate as to be released from my enforced and tedious amours by the hand of Providence, when Heaven willed it that I should overhaul the *San Lorenzo,* a brigantine bound for Seville, upon her return trip from Yucatan. This happened, through what I dare not miscall a coincidence, upon the tenth day of August, in the year of grace 1787—which, as I need hardly inform the devout, was the feast day of the brigantine's patron, St. Laurence of Huesca.

Aboard this ship I found the Princess Teresa Antonia de Bourbon, upon a pleasure jaunt amid the bright pomps which ordinarily surround royalty. She was a handsome, if rather large, young woman, then barely twenty-one years old; and her nominal father (who at this time was Prince of the Asturias) no long while afterward became King Charles the Fourth of Spain. Now that I verify the matter, because of my dislike for looseness no less in language than in behavior, his accession took place just four months and four days later. The question, in any case, remained open whether the true father of this princess had been Ortiz, or Pignatelli, or the Portuguese Count of Lancaster: for the morals of Queen Maria Luisa were such as no thoughtful Christian could dwell upon without reprobation. For this reason I dismiss the repugnant topic in silence.

Through this remarkable intervention of Providence, I repeat, the problem of my vicarious and unquiet home life was settled with decorum, now that I made of Teresa Antonia my mistress. I had no further need to be cluttering up my bedroom with unfamiliar, squalling young women. I could relax in comfort after our supper had been disposed of, and devote my evenings to a study of the best classic writers, now my appalled clients knew that, day in and day out, I compelled a royal princess to become the unhappy victim of my lasciviousness; for the performance was so noteworthy as to justify me in making it permanent.

Its hardihood served as an ever-present reminder, throughout the whole civilized world, of Gasparilla's intrepid ruthlessness; and even though she spoke with an unpleasantly harsh and manlike voice, and was urgent rather too often to be comforted by my amorous abilities, Teresa Antonia and I became honestly fond of each other.

But my heart remained faithful to Isabel de Castro.

8

So WIDESPREAD is human duplicity that very soon after my abduction of the princess I was approached by the governors of East Florida and of West Florida, in an attempt to ransom her. Their visit to my island kingdom was made in secret, because I ranked as their official enemy, and for a considerable while each one of them had offered a reward for my capture. Memory does not retain the exact amount, but it was tolerably flattering.

In point of fact, we during the third winter of my career had reached a gentleman's agreement by which

I paid to Don Manuel de Zespedes and Don Arturo O'Neill a pension, so that my islands should not be molested at any time during my absence upon professional excursions. Whensoever Gasparilla was in residence, I had told them, they were welcome enough to attack in full force; and they both laughed, a trifle ruefully, at the diverting notion of anybody's being so foolhardy.

Now, though, they, who affected to be my friends, came to Gasparilla Island, at His Most Catholic Majesty's order, to wheedle me into parting with Teresa Antonia, in exchange for a price insultingly higher than they had put upon me—and without pausing to reflect that my continued possession of a royal princess was an advertisement of my invincibility such as no thrifty pirate could afford upon any terms to relinquish.

Besides that, I rather enjoyed sleeping with the girl. I had become used to having her about; and for a royal personage, she was intelligent enough. Her temper was not over well-governed (as the reader may observe, alas, a little farther on in my narrative), but there is no denying that so far as went bedroom amenities, she had inherited a noble portion of her mother's ardor.

And so, while Teresa Antonia poured coffee for the three of us after dinner, I reproved O'Neill and Zespedes for their efforts to dismantle our domesticity. And I then dismissed them with a variety of well-chosen observations concerning the sanctity of home life such as at the moment happened to occur to me.

28

9

IN BRIEF, the King of Pirates continued to thrive upon a sound basis of fixed business principles, of panic terror, and of judicious advertising. We builded upon our islands more and yet more numerous and comfortable homes (through the materials and workmen that I got, in private, from O'Neill and Zespedes) until we had seven mansions, in the later Spanish Renaissance style, upon Cayo Costa; three upon Sanibel, including the rectory; and five upon Pine Island. My own residence, which was in the more impressive red and yellow Moorish manner, graced Gasparilla Island.

All these buildings were equipped, not unhandsomely, with furnishings borrowed from my clients' cowardice. I presided, in short, over a settlement as wealthy, for its modest dimensions, and as well conducted as you could have found anywhere in any other civilized and enlightened community.

My followers, by this time, had acquired forty-three wives, as well as well as seventeen children; and, in addition, we owned fifteen white menservants, eleven maidservants, thirty-two male Negroes, and if my memory serves me, some twenty probationary prisoners, who awaited their turn, in due course, to become free buccaneers. Meanwhile we employed them as gardeners and to keep clean our privies. We lodged them in a building upon Captiva Island, where there was also a cemetery.

Father Verdago provided against all our rather numerous religious needs, in the way of burials and christenings and confession and penances. His chapel (with a fine series of instructive and sanguinary windows in colored glass, which, as a delicate tribute to Teresa Antonia, commemorated the story of St. Laurence of Huesca and St. Hippolytus of Rome) was upon Sanibel Island, where every Sunday my followers attended divine worship in a body.

Upon this especial point I had need to be inflexible, inasmuch as a number of my men were not inclined to ensure their souls' salvation in the proper manner; but I saw to it that they did. As I told them with candor, we could not afford, in our touch-and-go profession, to provoke any celestial disfavor.

My adherence to correct principles in dealing with mankind and Heaven had been rewarded, meanwhile, to an edifying degree. My ledgers now showed that I had overhauled and taxed one hundred and thirty-six ships; of these, in the days of my nonage as a pirate, I had sunk twelve; nineteen ships had escaped me, through cowardice and their superior swiftness; and upon one occasion, as I elect to record with the frankness which befits a gentleman in dealing with his own shortcomings, an English war vessel, the *Pegasus*, put me to flight, with fourteen of my men killed and seventeen wounded.

This was my one serious setback, however, in all the impressive epic of Gasparilla's career; and during this brisk period, through the favor of Providence and my own ingenuity and vigilance, I had contrived to lay aside almost enough money to justify me in retiring from practice.

So with a glad heart I reverently made ready, under Heaven's will, to return to my adored Isabel, from whom (like that yet other world-famous mariner, King Odysseus, from his far more mildly cherished Penelope, I reflected) fate had dissevered me now for some seven years. The capture of but one more wealthy merchantman, according to my figures, might make up the deficit.

PART THREE

"*Who wins his love shall lose her,*
Who loses her shall gain,
For still the spirit woos her,
A soul without a stain;
And memory still pursues her
With longings not in vain."

IO

THE *Santa Clara*, then bound from Cadiz for St. Augustine, was the next ship which surrendered to me, in February, upon the feast day of my own Barcelona's notable saint, Eulalia; and my ensuing interview with the brig's captain proved satisfactory, for we met as one gentleman with another. To the best of my recollection, he was a native of Santander; and I found his politeness superior to criticism.

To be plundered by the great Gasparilla, Captain Ruiz was pleased to remark, he weighed as an experience untinged with dishonor; it was, rather, to his personal judgment, a mark of distinction; for the world knew that Gasparilla did not bother himself, nowadays, with any except the more handsome and noteworthy trading vessels.

When I had acknowledged his civility in befitting terms, and inquired what money he had aboard, he estimated the amount as some 10,000 pesos, which he produced in the form of canvas bags and laid upon the table of his own cabin.

"And I am the more free-handed in this matter," he added, with the engaging frankness of a forthright man of the world, "not simply because money is the root of all evil—"

"It is not becoming for us laymen to misquote the Holy Scriptures," I rebuked him—but without asperity —"which nowhere dispraise money. To the contrary, money is a defence, and money answers all, we are told in Ecclesiastes. And St. Paul declares only that a love for money is the root of much evil among persons who have strayed from the Christian faith. I infer that their misconduct need not concern a communicant during his transaction of business matters."

Captain Ruiz smiled, for some reason or another; but he said only:

"Here, in any case, dear sir, is metal in which I have not any share or interest. Don Diego de Arredondo must pay our toll, it appears."

"And who is this Don Diego?"

Tall Ruiz shrugged.

"I can tell you only," he assured me, "that I have been employed to convey him and his wife and his five sons to St. Augustine. He is badly crippled with rheumatism; the climate of Florida has been recommended as a specific; and he is related, in one or another degree, to the late Royal Engineer of Spain who rebuilded a great deal of St. Augustine, in Montiano's time, a good fifty

36

years ago. That much is certain. Upon the rumor that Don Diego is just as closely allied with Satan, I need not pass judgment. It is none of my business. And for the rest, it was only last Thursday that my men and I all drank to his health upon his seventieth birthday."

"Which I now fear must be the last of all my birthdays," another voice remarked, at this point; "and I regret the circumstance. Yes, Captain Gasparilla; for this world of ours is somewhat too droll—as this renewal of our acquaintance well testifies—for me to be quitting it willingly."

You may depend upon it that I regarded the speaker with some interest; for to the very best of my knowledge I had not ever before laid eyes upon him.

I I

HE WAS A FRAIL and benevolent-looking, white-haired old gentleman, attired in black and silver, who at this moment stood at the cabin's doorway, leaning upon an ebony cane. Behind him, one saw a short, stout woman, and about her clustered a bevy of gaping small boys, as I noted without any special attentiveness, now that the old man had glanced first at his moneybags upon the broad red-covered table, and then upward, across this same table, toward me, with intent, very bright eyes.

"You have my congratulations," he continued, as he seated himself, with the painstaking stiffness of a cripple, "upon the generosity which fortune has shown to-day toward your mother's son. I do not wholly begrudge this turn of events.—For it happens that I remember you as an infant in your cradle, my captain; we have both changed since then; but you are much like her."

"Why, now can it be, Don Diego de Arredondo, that you once knew my sainted mother?"

He replied: "I was so far honored, in Madrid, a while after her marriage. But it all happened a great long time ago. And so the details of our meeting evade me. I can remember only that the dusk had not yet fallen. The evening star at this time was Saturn. There was no other star to be seen in the grayish blue sky except only this one planet very close to a crescent moon. They were both directly above us; and about us were oleanders. We were both young."

His slow voice altered; and with a gesture of apology, he said,—

"It is odd that I should recall these trifles only; yet,

after all, it is not prudent for anybody's memory to be omniscient."

"And prudence," I reminded him, "is a pre-eminent virtue."

At that, Don Diego de Arredondo caressed his chin with the notably long fingers of his right hand, as he sat there smiling and looking upward.

"Why, but yes: for prudence gives sound advice, Captain Gasparilla. And so, this same prudence is now urging me to profit by time's passage. Yet we remain hidalgos, my captain. The code of an hidalgo does not permit discourtesy toward any gentlewoman. And in the elation of robbing me, you have failed to acknowledge my beloved wife's presence. You have omitted to remove your hat in homage to her so numerous perfections."

"My apologies, señora—" I began, with the most courtly of salutations.

I stopped short; and I daresay I gulped: for I found that this squat, homely, pudgy, kind-faced housewife was the former lodestar of my existence.

"And you did not know me!" she who had once been Isabel de Castro spoke, in reproof. "Oh, I do not question that I have become old and ugly since the last time we saw each other, whereas you, José, you simply remind me of a green bay tree, with hardly a line in your face. I mean the one in the Book of Psalms; and I do think you might have been more tactful about it."

"It is merely," I replied, "that the loveliness which I

39

left in bud has now reached a stupefying maturity. And besides that, Isabel, you must make allowances for the not unnatural confusion of my faculties at this dreadful moment. Now that I find you with a husband and as many as five children, I cannot but doubt if you have remained wholly faithful to me."

"But it has been good gracious only knows how long since you deserted me, José, and took to evil courses, with not even one letter—"

"It has been seven years," I began, "since because of my not ever swerving adoration and fond faith—"

But the affable, fat little creature had gone on talking resistlessly, with a complacent flavor of extreme self-admiration, saying:

"—And I did wait quite faithfully, for a great long while, because I was always very fond of you, and in fact, ever since we were children, in your dear mother's day, as you ought to remember. She really did have the most beautiful head of hair that I ever saw in my life, with that natural wave to it. And so I kept hoping you would give up being a pirate and come back to me with the 500,000 pesos which you had promised—"

"I cannot grant, Isabel, that you waited quite faithfully for a great long while, inasmuch as during the passing of but seven years you have managed to acquire five strapping children."

"Yes, but then the last two of them—I mean Lucas and Antonio, of course, and as you can see for yourself —were twins. It might happen to anybody."

"That does not very much alter matters," was my reply; "and I do not reproach you, O my heart's dearest. But it seems to me an odd thing that only five minutes ago I had complete faith in you. That faith has enabled me to devote an untiring industry to the pursuit of a profession not without its repugnant aspects. That faith has heartened me to endure the hardships and the unfriendly criticism which necessarily attend the practice of piracy, so that I might lay aside the 500,000 pesos which would ensure for us the cosy villa and the unending felicity of which I had dreamed always until but five minutes ago."

I paused then; I sighed, rather creditably; and I pointed toward the cabin table, saying:

"To-day the desired sum is made up. The final fraction of it lies here between us in the form of your husband's moneybags. And to-day, even in the same instant that I attain success, I find you have not kept faith. I face the unarguable proofs that, even after one has made an appropriate allowance for twins, you have been false to me upon four occasions. And it is not across these piled up moneybags I am looking at you, my lost Isabel, but across the grave of my youth."

Here I was interrupted by a gentle cough.

"The situation is no doubt distressing from your point of view," Don Diego observed, "but it does not justify the intrusion into a lofty prose passage of any reference to the grave of your youth. Poets have been looking at this and that and the other phenomenon

41

across the grave of their youth for so long a while that the simile has become moth-eaten."

"My anguish at this instant," I replied, "is far too unbridled for me to dally with the refinements of rhetoric."

"Even so, my captain, a checkrein for that unbridled anguish of yours has occurred to me—"

"And may I inquire its nature, Don Diego?"

He waved his long-fingered hand.

"The matter is delicate. An adjustment between a husband and the lover of his wife—as your tall blond father would assure you, my captain, if only he still lived—is not easily arranged in public. Now Captain Ruiz, I am certain, would find tedious the discussion of affairs in which he has no least personal interest. And as for you, my love"—he addressed Isabel fondly—"I am making bold to suggest that, in common with your offspring, you may find the view from the ship's deck to be both instructive and agreeable."

She answered him, with a condescension which was not unfriendly, by declaring:

"If you had any sense whatever, Diego, you would not think, no, not for one solitary instant, that I was going to leave you at the mercy of an unprincipled pirate, quite apart from your rheumatism's making you helpless, and even though I do have to ask your pardon, José, for saying it before your face, but your hands reek with blood. I do not mean, of course, that they need washing just now; but only in a manner of speak-

42

ing: because your infamy has become so extensive that people are always asking me, in the most embarrassing sort of way, however I could have thought about you as an at all possible husband."

"The susceptibility of youth—" I began.

"Of course," Isabel continued, fair-mindedly, "it is none of their business; and besides that, how could I have imagined you would turn out to be a criminal with a woodcut of you in the public gazettes? I must have cut out a half-dozen at the very least. Still, they do ask, over and over again, especially Anita. She is Diego's sister, you know, only you probably would not, besides her having married again. She is a countess now, and not anybody is allowed to forget the fact, I can assure you. What I mean is that you used to have such nice eyes."

Her voice changed then. Her hand touched my hand; and the absurd creature said,—

"Oh, my own dear José!"

You would not think a fat little married woman could be so shameless in the presence of her alert, forever smiling husband.

"Let us say farewell for the present, my love," Don Diego exhorted, incisively.

I 2

"You perceive she is still fond of you," Don Diego de Arredondo continued, now that the two of us were alone. "Women, as some philosopher or another has remarked, are unconscionably loyal creatures. He was no doubt a bachelor. At all events, this unmanly trait simplifies matters. You have merely, I submit, to make my wife a widow in order to be rid, once and for all, of your unbridled anguish. Your adored Isabel will be at your disposal, as well as somewhat more than that modest competence which was your other fixed goal; and the pair of you can at once set about living happily forever afterward in the approved style of romance."

I shuddered at the notion; but I concealed my abhorrence courteously.

"Don Diego," I answered, with reproach, "there is no person breathing who more carefully honors romance now that, to the general public, Gasparilla has become a figure of romance. But it is not right of you to suggest that I should murder a friend of my sainted mother, in order to marry his widow and to set about the rearing of five infant stepsons. Your murder, in itself, I admit, would strike no discordant note; it would be criticized with disfavor by nobody; but the proposed sequel would be injudicious."

"And for what reason, Gasparilla?"

"Why, but you must remember, sir," I explained, "that in the world's eyes I figure as a desperado who excels in all branches of infamy. I cannot afford to subdue the lively and remunerative horror with which all merchantmen regard the King of Pirates, through subsiding into domestic life at any such wholesale rate as five small stepchildren. The proceeding would be ludicrous. It would be the ruin of my career."

"But then, to the other side," says Don Diego, "have you the right to disregard some yet other requirements than those of your ruthlessness, and to abandon the fine ideals which have guided you toward distinction in crime? You would not ever have taken up piracy, I must make bold to remind you, nor would you have become world-famous—with a half-dozen woodcuts of you in the public gazettes—if you had not been inspired by love for my wife."

He paused at this point. He said then:

"But, no! for here I find need to distinguish. You have been inspired, rather, by the girl whom I too loved, and whom I married, while you at a discreet distance continued to adore her."

"Ah, yes; for she was wholly beautiful, was she not, Don Diego?"

"There was never, to my not narrow experience," said he, "any young woman more lovely, or more sympathetic, or endowed with a disposition more amiable, than was the girl whom time has transformed into my wife."

"In brief, Don Diego, she was perfection. And I have lost her forever—not simply upon account of the excellent taste which she displayed in marrying you, sir, inasmuch as your decease, I can but repeat, could be arranged without inconvenience, but because the brightly colored small goddess whom I adored does not any longer exist."

"And I too have lost her forever, child, now that I have been married to Isabel for a considerable while. At the back of my mind, I believe the main danger of any marriage is that, no matter what sort of person you may lead to the altar, you must by-and-by find yourself married to a quite different person. As a rule, I do not talk about this belief. It is a phenomenon which the wise husband observes silently."

"Oh, but very truly we are companions in misfortune, Don Diego, and you have my sympathy, now that I have seen your esteemed wife and your five fine children."

"You mistake matters, Gasparilla, because for an Arredondo it would not be difficult to regain that which

46

has gone out of our hand-to-mouth existence into the land without shadows."

"Now whatever in this world can you be talking about, Don Diego?"

"Why, but I am not talking about anything in this world," he answered; "or rather, to be wholly accurate, I am talking about this carved green stone which I wear as a watch fob. I employ the green stone in this fashion because it makes the time that which one prefers to have it. And I am talking also about the odd fact that I do not any longer take a deep interest in such kickshaws now that I have faced the great magic of marriage."

"I do not question, Don Diego, that marriage is a holy institution, inasmuch as one finds everywhere its martyrs; but when you term it a magic I have not the happiness to detect your meaning."

He replied gravely: "Nor can I make clear to you my meaning, because such incomplete persons as are bachelors and spinsters may not hope to understand this affair. I can tell you only that being married is a very strong magic.

"As you have noticed, even in the teeth of your rhetoric"—he resumed, with a smile which appeared slightly derisive—"that dumpy and unimportant-looking little woman who has just left us has no longer any special physical charms. I too have noted this. I have noted likewise that her intelligence is not brilliant. Her talking rambles so that I cannot always guess at what she is talking about. Her disposition, so far as I am concerned, is to be deplored, inasmuch as she invariably speaks both to and about me with an unexplained resentment—and yet, too, as if I were only a half-witted child who must be indulged. In fact, I am tolerably certain that, at heart, my wife does think about me as being the least gifted and by long odds the least attractive of her children."

The age-stricken hidalgo shrugged, with an acrid resignation. He then continued:

"And yet, Gasparilla, my devotion to her is complete. There is no power upon earth which could persuade me to exchange this irrational and uncomely and so continually fault-finding person for the lovely and gentle young Isabel whom you and I thought perfect. And for that reason, my lad, this watch fob is at your disposal should you dare to use it."

"Still, sir, you are pleased to speak in riddles; and I can but ask what is your meaning, Don Diego?"

He answered me, speaking at some length, with a sort of leisured amusement. And that I do not record this part of his talking is a reticence which, as my readers may observe later, is prompted by philanthropy. His talking would have appalled most persons; but by every one of my historians the fact has been noted that Gasparilla remained a stranger to fear of any kind.

So I put to him a question; and he answered it with an appearance of frankness.

"Then our agreement is concluded," I returned; "and that my gratitude toward you excels description, my actions shall now attest. In the normal course of affairs, it would have been my duty to remove from this table one half of your moneybags. But you, Don Diego, apart from being a strong buckler against the honor of my being married to your wife, have promised to become my benefactor in a manner how very far more striking! I take pleasure, sir, in exempting you from my customary tax rate; and even though I am now put to the sad necessity of accepting from you 2000 pesos, as a debt of honor—"

"I object," he declared, with a continuing in his amused gravity, "to the evaluation put upon Isabel. It is too low; it is humiliating: and in simple courtesy you ought to be demanding the final coin which lies here between us, in addition to a promissory note—"

"Your protest does you credit, Don Diego, for all that you speak in the heat of miscomprehension. I do not pretend to evaluate the lady who shares your bed and affections. It is merely that I promised your wife I would be possessed of 500,000 pesos when I next saw her; I have in hand, it so happens, but 498,000 pesos; and I cannot agree to have Gasparilla figure as a braggart liar. The code of an hidalgo, to which you referred just now, when I had my hat on, does not allow him to break faith with any person to whom he has given his word of honor."

"I comprehend," he returned; "and Gasparilla's acute sense of honor, upon the whole, is very well worth my money."

13

It came about in this way that, upon our return to Gasparilla Island, when the March of 1791 was running out with an unusual raw, bright bluster, I found it my unavoidable duty to provide for the future of Teresa Antonia.

I could not liberate her, because she knew a great deal too much about the affairs of our pirate colony, after having enjoyed my favor and confidence for so long a while; but I told the girl that I would permit her to keep, as her dowry, all the jewels and the expensive clothes which, during the last three years and seven months, I had bestowed upon her, with that innate and regal generosity which so very many students of my character have declared to be one of my numerous fine traits.

Modesty prevents me, as my readers may notice, from endorsing the correctness of this verdict. I merely mention it.

But to clip the tale of my kindness: I authorized Teresa Antonia to pick out whichever one of my men she might prefer as her husband. I would see to it, I explained, that he married her out-of-hand. Should she elect to make happy any of my already married followers—a course against which, in the behalf of morality, I felt it needful to advise her, in a dispassionate yet friendly manner—why, but even then I stood ready to strain this point, because of my exceedingly deep interest in her welfare. The man's current wife, I assured Teresa Antonia, would be disposed of.

In brief, I offered every agreeability that prudence could allow, because of my wish to end our relations politely and to restore my now superfluous mistress to a more honorable way of living.

She said fiercely, "And so you have tired of me, also!"

"No person of good taste could ever weary of your charms, alike of mind and body, my dear love," I answered her, with a painstaking and complete civility. "It is merely that I am going upon a journey; and before departing, I feel it is my duty to see you settled in comfort and equipped with a trustworthy husband to protect you. I cannot leave you at loose ends, my pet, among buccaneers who, while I have found them to be sound associates in business, are not blessed with impeccant morals in dealing with attractive young women."

She replied, I regret to say, by calling me a long-winded hypocrite. And the tall termagant went on speaking hoarsely and with animation, for a loud while, as to my perfidy and insolence and heartlessness and my shortcomings in general.

It is a comfort to remember that, with the unruffled courtesy which many persons have been so kind as to admire in my deportment, I remained patient under this unmerited abuse, until, of a sudden, Teresa Antonia had whipped out a dagger and stabbed me twice, in the left shoulder, but a little distance above my heart.

An attack so unlooked for did nettle me, I confess, into a moment of anger, during which I acted, it is possible, without pausing for sufficient reflection.

No one of us, however, can control his temper in all conditions; and I deplored quite honestly the unpleasing spectacle of Teresa Antonia lying dead at my feet, even though I had shot her without any special premeditation, and at an instant when she was trying to murder her benefactor. She was a superb woman, upon the grand scale, with the most beautiful thighs and bosom I have ever seen anywhere; and her companionship had been to me upon Gasparilla Island an unfailing solace.

In brief, I was fond of her. I still cherish the memory of Teresa Antonia de Bourbon, who was the daughter of a queen; and I would not record in this place the unhappy results of her irritable disposition were it not for the absurd way in which the girl's decease has been misrepresented by scandal-mongers. The report is still current that, while in a state of drunkenness, great Gasparilla unsheathed his unconquerable sword and, without warning, in mere petulance, struck off the head of his Spanish princess.

That any such behavior (apart from seeming a physical impossibility) would be inconsistent with my well-known courtesy toward members of the gentle sex, I need hardly point out to you, my reflective reader; and besides, I was not wearing a sword at the moment of my fair young friend's regretted death. I used one of the two pistols which at all times I carried at my belt; and moreover, I was entirely sober.

But it is thus that falsehood follows after distinguished persons, and at every period has delighted to traduce the world's greater heroes, through the mob's envy of their superiority in virtue and high achievements.

14

Upon the last day of April, at a quarter past two in the afternoon (for I remember noticing the Cathedral sundial), I came into the Plaza of the city of St. Augustine, dressed in plain, serviceable gray, and bearing the pack of a pedlar.

Nor would I, who abhor vainglory, have my readers suppose that, in visiting thus privately (like a monarch who travels incognito) the stronghold of my most bitter enemies, I displayed an especial sample of the intrepidity with which historians have seen fit to accredit Gasparilla's heroism at all times. According to the strict letter of the law, I was due to be hanged should anyone recognize me. To the other side, it was past human conception that even the King of Pirates could be so dauntless as to enter St. Augustine unprotected; yet furthermore, there was the Governor to be considered.

—For, as I have noted elsewhere, my relationship with the Governor of East Florida, as well as with the Governor of West Florida, although informal, was wholly friendly; and each one of these gentlemen appreciated the neat pension which I paid to him so that the three of us might live amicably. I thus knew that even in the unlikely event of my being apprehended, my friend Don Manuel de Zespedes would adhere to his public duty by locking me up in the Castillo, and see to his own private interest by effecting my escape.

So with an untroubled conscience I disguised myself, aboard the *Gasparilla*, as a pedlar; and I came ashore, just south of Matanzas Inlet, no great while after breakfast, fetching with me two of our Negro slaves. I do not recall their names. They carried spades and an oak chest containing, as I did not conceal from my crew, our quarterly payment to the Governor of East Florida, which I intended to bury in a spot he had designated. This, inasmuch as we could not communicate with each other publicly, was my usual method of conveying to him his pension.

I then arranged with Roderigo Lopez, as my lieutenant, for the *Gasparilla* to await my arrival, within ten days at utmost, in the harbor of Fernandina; and the sloop sailed northward.

After the ship's departure I travelled with the two Negroes a little distance inland, turning away from the sea marshes into a thick, huge jungle of palms and sage trees and live oaks,—among which, under the relentless spring sun of Florida, our progress so steadily increased in difficulty, and in a surplus of perspiration and mosquitoes, that through compassion for my attendants I resolved to let them suffer no longer.

I paused beside a notably large live oak. I told my two Negroes to bury the chest where we then were, and whence the Governor could fetch it at leisure. The stout, faithful fellows obeyed me with alacrity; and with my customary reluctance in all such affairs, I shot each one of them through the head when their labors had neared completion, about a half-hour, or it may have been some forty minutes, later. My watch I had left aboard the *Gasparilla*, as being of too large value for a pedlar to be wearing.

I found it a comfort to observe that both of my assistants entered into the presence of their Maker without any very visible signs of agony. Their bodies I dragged back to the seashore; and relinquished them to the waters of the ocean. I then finished the work of these unfortunate Africans, who had perished untimely at an interminable distance from their homes and loved ones; I marked the tree with my case knife; and I covered the newly digged earth with broken branches, the most of which I obtained from sage trees.

Having thus deposited a reserve fund against future needs, in a place which now remained unknown to any person alive except only myself, I went onward to the west; and soon reached the Kings Road between New Smyrna and St. Augustine. I trudged northward upon this noble highway, observing to the left of me tall, moss-hung forests that were more ancient than Abraham of Mamre (for such was the pious turn of my reflections), and having to my right a sleek and sunlit ocean which the canons of my Church assured me to be five days older than Eden.

I admired with a grateful heart the natural beauties which to every side of me, in this second Eden that we call Florida, had been provided lavishly by the sublime Father of all mankind; and I saw to it likewise that, whenever I met or was passed by any of my human brethren upon the highway, my reloaded pistols were kept hidden by the gray smock I was wearing, so as not to unsettle the peace of mind of my fellow creatures in a world thus unmistakably designed for a Christian's contentment.

56

When I came to the San Sebastian River, I passed over the Bridge of the Sea Cows unhindered; and I walked into the city of St. Augustine and came to its Plaza, by way of King Street, without any shadow of inconvenience except only my increasing hunger. This led me to dine first of all (at a small tavern in the side street of San Carlos, where the fried shrimp were uncommonly appetizing, I remember), before I went back to the Plaza.

In the Plaza I unpacked my wares. At the Cathedral door I made several sales of my knickknacks to townspeople who would. have died of terror if only they could have known that they haggled with great Gasparilla. This reflection very much pleased me.

When trade dwindled I left the Plaza. I passed toward the gaily clad, fair gentlewomen and their nobly born escorts who, for the sake of coolness, were strolling beside the sea-wall, upon the esplanade called La Marina. The all-dreaded King of Pirates went with a smiling obsequiousness among these chattering, empty-headed weaklings, with a pedlar's pack hung about the neck which everybody within eyeshot would have delighted to see decorated with a noose; and I came in this way, without hindrance, to the Castillo de San Marcos, just as the Cathedral bells behind me announced the current hour to be five o'clock in the afternoon.

15

AT THE CASTILLO DE SAN MARCOS, Don Diego awaited my arrival, upon one of the five benches set at a little distance from the moat of the castle, well shaded by cedar trees and overlooking the broad Matanzas River. This was now at low tide, I remember, so that many white seagulls were at supper upon the exposed brown patches of sand among the blue water.

I found the old gentleman in excellent spirits; for the magic-laden air of Florida, he assured me, had well-nigh banished his rheumatism since our last meeting. He could now walk almost briskly, with the aid of his gold-headed ebony cane, which reposed beside him against the weather-beaten gray bench; and he hoped, the old man declared, in due course of time to become a centenarian here in St. Augustine, before being buried in the Cemetery of Nombre de Dios.

"But your affair comes first, Gasparilla," he resumed

affably; "so let us defer my interment for this after-noon."

And he then began to talk about the green stone in the watch fob he was still wearing.

The stone had been bequeathed to him, so he now told me, by his lamented because deceased half-brother, Antonio de Arredondo—and with this name (inasmuch as I had been inquiring about the Arredondo family) I admitted myself to be not unfamiliar.

"—For, as I recall it, Don Diego, he was that Royal Engineer of Spain who, when the English were stealing Georgia, rebuilded and refortified the Castillo just behind us. He likewise enclosed the city of St. Augustine within what I have always felt to be the insecure defence of a hedge, to keep out the English."

"Why, but yes, Gasparilla; and yet, just somehow, no English army was ever able to get through his hedge of that plant which we call the Spanish bayonet."

"Even so, sir, the correct name is *Yucca aloifolia*; and for that reason—"

"But I am not concerned with reason, you forever posturing child! I am concerned, rather, with the two facts, that his hedge was cut down by Don Melchor Feliu, as being a nuisance and a foolish superstition, in 1762; and that during the following year the English at long last entered St. Augustine."

"—And your brother built the City Gates, which still stand—"

I broke off short. I asked by-and-by,—

"Was it about those gates you were talking upon the *Santa Clara*?"

"Yes, Gasparilla; but then, to the other side, do you remember, I may have been talking a deceitful nonsense because of my strong need to get out of your clutches. You forget, my child, that you are the most formidable sort of desperado. You terrify all beholders. And besides that, it is to my interest to be rid of you, because of your romantic infatuation for my wife," he added, with a somewhat impish grin. "So in your place, I would not trust me."

"Ah, but I do trust you, Don Diego, on account of —let us say—your fond memories of my sainted mother."

The old gentleman regarded me pensively.

"Sometimes," he remarked, in an unaccountably aggrieved manner, "you display gleams of intelligence!"

Afterward he said, drily: "She was not without successors in my esteem; for the heart of an Arredondo is an inn with many patrons. At all events, I may tell you that mechanical engineering was not the sole art which my accomplished half-brother practiced. He so arranged matters that his castle could not ever be captured, or his hedge broken through, by any enemy; and that his gates could be made to open otherwise than upon the road which leads to the Cemetery of Nombre de Dios, just north of St. Augustine. —Or so, at least, he told me. Yet all this would imply sorcery; and learned persons do not any longer believe in such out-of-date nonsense."

"But I, Don Diego, am not a learned person—"

"Yet, Gasparilla, you ought to remember—"

"—Although I am tolerably familiar, it is true, with the main body of Spanish and French and English and Italian literature—"

"Nevertheless, Gasparilla—"

"—And I have read, of course, all the best classic writers; but only in Latin, sir. For Greek authors, I have had to depend upon translations—"

"That is regrettable, Gasparilla; but even so—"

"—And I have likewise studied the Holy Scriptures, along with five volumes of commentaries, and the lives of the major saints, and most of what remains to us of Provençal poetry. But that appears to be about all, sir, apart from naval tactics and a fair working knowledge of medicine and heraldry, because in my profession one does not have very much time for reading. So, to be brief with you, Don Diego, I dare not pretend to be a learned person; and I am determined to leave St. Augustine by way of the City Gates."

"The departure of the King of Pirates," Don Diego answered, "may well prove to St. Augustine, and to both of the Floridas, a not unwelcome event. It is my duty, as a loyal subject to the King of Spain, to weigh this circumstance. I am not certain but that upon yet other grounds it would be a blessing to humankind at large," he added, reflectively. "Even so, my boy, I am so humble-minded that this present world contents me. But you, Gasparilla, you are more heroic; and like

Alexander of Macedon, you demand new worlds to conquer."

He had me there. So I answered him with contrition, saying:

"It is my nature, sir, to overcome all opponents, that is true. Yet I could not very well have avoided this congenital trait. And it is because of this same trait that I am now inclined to retire from piracy by way of the City Gates. —For this relentless inheritance has compelled me to ascend to the top of my profession. Now that I have attained to this, as it were, enforced pre-eminence, it is not possible—no, not even for me, as I admit humbly—to add to the glory of Gasparilla."

"You have my sympathy, child; and your humility does you credit."

"Yet furthermore, sir," I continued, "my name has become so famous and my fairness in the practice of my profession is admired so widely, that all merchant vessels surrender, nowadays, at the first glimpse of my ensign. It follows that wealth pours in upon me endlessly. My opulence has become a plague, because it accumulates with a rapidity so far in excess of my power to dispose of it. I have come to detest the sight of the money of all nations; gems irritate me; and ingots provoke nausea."

"From all which, Gasparilla, I can but infer that when, upon the *Santa Clara*, you declared your worldly possessions to be limited to 498,000 pesos, you must have been treating candor with some parsimony."

"Ah, but that, sir, was a business transaction; and besides, I meant only my cash in hand. In talking for the first time with a stranger, whose honesty remained problematic, it would not have been prudent for me to mention the treasure hoards which I have buried throughout Florida. I may now tell you, my dear friend, that the peninsula is honeycombed with my wealth."

"You surprise me, my dear friend," he returned.

"Why, but it was only this morning, Don Diego, that through mere force of habit, I buried 20,000 pesos, according to my usual routine, immediately across the river, in a plantation of lime trees, upon Anastasia Island."

This was not quite the truth as to where I had hidden my treasure chest; but I did not wish to put upon my infirm benefactor the labor of digging up this money.

"Even so—" the old gentleman began.

"And now that I speak of routine, sir," I interrupted him, "I must tell you that, upon every one of these occasions, I am forced to dispose of my employees. I am compelled to defend myself against their possible lack of sound moral principles such as would prevent them from returning in secret to make off with my property. The monotony of these unavoidable precautions is becoming tedious."

Don Diego said, "But, you young cut-throat—!"

"You wrong me, sir," I protested; "for my nature is alike benevolent and tidy. So in all such affairs I use pistols. But to get on with my story: there is not in the

63

life of a too prosperous buccaneer any variety or excitement. I cannot any longer put up with the humdrum regularity of piratic existence; and for this reason, among other motives, I am determined to reform, irretrievably, in the companionship which you have promised to me."

"Very well, then," says Don Diego; "your desire for self-reformation, whatsoever may be its cause, is of a highly admirable nature; and as the friend of your infancy, I feel that it is my duty to assist you in departing from your present way of living, as well as—if indeed such altruism should prove humanly possible—to put an end to your talking."

16

So IN THE UPSHOT Don Diego de Arredondo went with me that night to the City Gates. We were alone there, in the bright moonlight of what he called Walburga's Eve, although it was really the feast day of St.

Catherine of Siena which was then drawing toward midnight.

He gave to me the green stone, and he performed a ceremony about which I am forced by prudence to remain silent; but it was followed by a result yet more strange, for I now saw that the woodlands beyond the open gates, and the palm-sheltered wide road which led toward the Cemetery of Nombre de Dios, were no longer lighted by the moon. It was as if, already, another day had begun there; and its dawn was rose-colored.

I was not afraid; but I thought it better to pass onward through the gates without stopping to think about the duplicity of many forms of magic working.

I looked back for a last glimpse of Don Diego. He waited there, in that very bright moonlight which did not extend beyond the City Gates. Behind him, I observed the deserted-looking houses, and the balconies projecting above the sidewalks, of narrow, wholly quiet, black and silver St. George Street.

He stood, I remember, a little hunched forward, leaning upon his ebony cane; but with his left hand he waved to me affably, in silence. I noticed that beside Don Diego now stood a tall young man who was dressed like a pedlar; and he likewise waved to me as if in farewell.

Afterward I heard somebody quite close to me declare,—

"It must have been the ham."

PART FOUR

"In dreams she grows not older
The lands of Dream among,
Though all the world wax colder,
Though all the songs be sung,
In dreams doth he behold her
Still fair and kind and young."

17

"WHY, BUT YES, José," my mother was saying, "it must have been the ham which turned you into a pirate."

My mother was always sweet about it after I had been bad; and you could depend upon her, too, in almost no time at all, to find out some good grown-up reason which showed that I had not really been bad, but just more or less thoughtless. It followed that my mother continued, with self-reproach:

"Yes, dear, I am quite certain it must have been the ham. And I ought to have known better than to let you have three whole slices of it at supper. So it was not your fault—or at least, not exactly, you small cannibal."

"But, mother, it did not seem like a dream. It was real. And I most certainly was a pirate—"

"And to think how nicely you got over it, the minute you waked up! You ought to be extremely thankful, José, that you waked up in good time to be nine years

69

old and to escape being hanged for your so numerous crimes," she informed me gravely.

"Yes, but, mother—well, but here is the green stone. You can see it yourself."

She looked at it—carelessly at first, and then with more interest.

"I do not know where you found this watch fob, José, but I remember a person who had one which was rather like it. It does not matter. And to him it never did matter!"

Afterward my mother said, in the sort of more happy voice she usually talked in:

"What really matters, José, is that it is time for breakfast. So you had best be getting ready for breakfast, my own dear little King of Pirates," she added, as she patted me ever so lightly upon the cheek.

And I knew she was right about my not ever having been a pirate and killing people and stealing their money. My mother was always right. I put aside the green stone, along with my clean socks, in the top bureau drawer. I washed all over, and behind both ears, in my dark green, round tin tub—only, it was painted a sort of cream color inside—and after that, I dressed myself, all by myself, just as I had been doing for months now, and ever since last summer, when Serafina died. She was my nurse. She went straight to paradise, I am certain.

For breakfast we had figs. I was allowed to dip them in sugar, and nothing ever tasted any better.

"Only, you must not eat but five of them," my mother said. "They will make your mouth sore. And besides that, if you continue to be a pig, you may get punished by being turned back into a pirate."

"Has the boy been dreaming again?" says my father.

"He is always dreaming," said my mother, "as you ought to know very well."

"And I know, too, my darling, that he must inherit this regrettable habit from the Cayo Costas, or from some other line upon your side of the family," my father returned, "for we Gasparillas do not waste time in dreaming."

My mother merely smiled. She was always a considerate wife.

18

My FATHER DID NOT MEAN so much the sort of dreams you have at night as what people call daydreams. He did not approve of my sitting still and just thinking about things in general.

"You had far better go outdoors, José, and play at something, somewhere," he would suggest, in his customary polite, vague manner.

"Yes, father dear," I would reply meekly.

Then he would return to his reading. I would go to some other part of our house. In this way we were both satisfied.

My father was always reading except when he was writing. He was writing a book. His book was going to be, after it got finished, A History of Provençal Poetry, with Metrical Translations of Its More Important Examples. I think that he really lived in Provence rather than in our house.

Our house was at the top of a hill, and there were a lot of big bushes and small trees around our house, and it was next to the Castros' house. Our house was all gray outside, but theirs was red and white, with some new window blinds, because they had more money than we had.

My father liked to talk to the Castros, and to everybody else, about his book, and the people who would be in it; and he did not seem to believe that anything which had happened since the thirteenth century was very important.

I suspect that, inside, my mother was not upon wholly cordial terms with Provençal poetry; but whenever my father talked about it, she listened as if she thought it to be a most interesting and entirely new subject. My mother, I can but repeat, was a considerate wife; and

72

for any woman to be that implies a fair amount of hypocrisy.

When his own father died, my father had inherited a rather large estate. Almost all of this he had got rid of, in manners as to which nobody, but especially my father, had any very clear notion. So, although we were descended from a number of once famous Gasparillas (and upon my mother's side, from the Cayo Costas), we were poor.

We did not worry concerning this circumstance. Neither one of my parents, I am certain, ever thought about money except as a thing which, when you had it, you spent. If you lacked it, you had only to sign a paper which the notary brought up from out of the village in spectacles, or to sell some of the furniture with worm holes in it, or some of my mother's jewelry, or a piece of my father's land; for then, at once, without any least trouble, you again had money.

I do not imagine the world ever saw a more thriftless couple. Yet, inasmuch as they were content, and I shared in their contentment, I cannot imagine, either, to what more intelligent use they could have devoted the old fine belongings of the Gasparillas and the Cayo Costas. With such things my parents bought happiness for all three of us. I can conceive of no better investment.

19

Captain Sanibel did not think that we ought to be happy without doing anything about it. Captain Sanibel was my godfather. Whenever I was not feeling well, I took all my medicines out of the silver spoon which he had given to me when I was christened. It had my initials on the end of it, in big curly letters.

When my father was not much older than I was, a small Captain Sanibel had been his schoolmate, a long way off from our house, at Oporto. I liked Captain Sanibel very much; but he worried me when I tried to think about him when he was only my size and did not have black, huge whiskers. He could not have looked like himself.

Captain Sanibel had been to all sorts of places in the geography, such as Greece and Cuba and Norway and Florida; and if you asked him to, very politely, and climbed up into his lap, then he would tell you about the big elephants and the witches and the unicorns who lived in these places; but in no one of these places had

74

Captain Pedro Olmos y de Sanibel ever learned how to speak without being completely certain about everything.

"You are heading for ruin, Clemente," he would declare to my father, "with your continual selling and mortgaging and borrowing and your continual writing in a corner. Nobody, to begin with, cares about your Propontic poets—"

"Provençal," said my father, mildly; "and the interest among scholars, as to this unique body of literature, is considerable."

"Yet scholars, my dear Clemente, do not have any money with which to buy your book, even if you could find anywhere a publisher who was fool enough to print it. But at court there is always an appointment or some office for a Gasparilla. You are still remembered at court, you soft-spoken reprobate, among a large number of great ladies. They would like nothing better than to have you compromising them again. They have influence; and our Heavenly Father, it is said, preserves His omnipotence by not ever opposing anything which a woman wishes. You would be well provided for at court."

"But I do not like living at court, Pedro. I used to. But I found there were too many women about."

"You might very easily," the friendly captain pursued, "get back into the good graces of the Princess of the Asturias. She has by no means forgotten you, I wager. Your future would then be assured. And when she becomes Queen of Spain, you could have me made an admiral. It is not right of you, Clemente, to neglect my welfare."

"Yet I have heard, Pedro, that only last month she brought forth another baby, so that her need for service cannot be immediate."

"Why, but yes," said the captain. "It is a girl, this time; and they are calling it, I believe, Teresa Antonia. This one is Lancaster's, they tell me. But that does not matter; for the Princess does not intend to falter in well-doing, with still other collaborators. And so, as I was saying, at court both you and your most lovely wife—"

"And as I was saying, Pedro, I do not like living at court," my father returned.

He then rumpled up his thin, light yellow hair with both of his hands; and he went on talking lazily, with his white hands clasped behind his small, blond head.

"As concerns Juanita," says he, "if we went back to court, then yet again I would be annoyed by the men who made love to her. A husband is compelled, by popular prejudice, to resent these attempts at seduction. And so, the last time that we were in Madrid, for example, I had to fight a duel with the younger Arredondo on account of the attention he paid her. We were both wounded. The entire affair was most disagreeable. Why upon earth should I be expected to exchange pistol shots with intelligent persons who display the good taste to fall in love with my wife?"

76

"I assume that your question is rhetorical," said the captain, stiffly.

"Why, but not at all," my father assured him. "Now you, Pedro, enjoy fighting. It is your profession to fire large guns at complete strangers, and to have them shoot back at you. But for my part, I prefer to live here in quiet at Montserrat, and to get on with my work."

"It is not work which will provide for the boy here," Captain Sanibel retorted, patting my head, "because at this rate you by-and-by will be leaving him a penniless orphan."

"You have promised to get him into the Navy," my father said, "and that will provide for him. I daresay he will get on quite nicely in the Navy."

20

IN BRIEF, my father was wholly selfish and, in consequence, wholly charming. He made himself agreeable to everybody, because he disliked to associate with people, and with women especially, who were not in a complacent frame of mind. But I do not think that he cared deeply about any person, during the time I knew him, except only his dead Provençal poets.

To my mother, for example, he was far more than courteous. He agreed she was right about everything. He told her incessantly how well she was looking to-day, and how very becoming was her hat, or her gown, or her mantilla, or something else she was wearing. He protested, as if in real dismay, whenever she had brushed back her crinkly brown hair so that it did not cover the tops of her ears, because, he said, this made her some-what less beautiful.

He did not call her Juanita, but darling; and I re-member how the tall, thin, handsome, but vaguely languid man always arose from his chair when she came into the room, as well as what a ceremony he would make of arranging my mother's chair for her in our din-ing-room at every meal. It was all quite as if he were her lover instead of her husband. But at bottom, I now believe, he looked upon her as being a highly useful person who attended to his housekeeping, and so en-abled him to go on with his writing in comfort.

I did not think about my father in any vein so criti-cal during the time that he and my mother and I were happy together. I knew then that my father was the most learned person in the whole world. And I liked him, too; for even though he did not spoil me quite so actively as did my mother, yet toward me he exhibited a never-failing, grave courtesy; and he addressed me, almost always, as if I were his equal in age.

I did not suspect that, for a father, this was unusual. I knew only that, in addition to his having read everything which had ever been printed in any book, my father was interesting to listen to when he talked about his Provençal poets.

No other child at the age of nine, I imagine, has ever been so familiar with Provençal poets. I thought about them, to every intent, as being people I knew, like the Castros, or Estevan, the blacksmith's boy, or Dr. Genêt. It would not have surprised me if at any moment Geoffrey Rudel, or Raimbaut de Vaqueiras, or Pierre Vidal, had ridden up the hill, and among the hibiscus and cactus plants and lemon trees of our front yard, to see what my father was writing about him. And in private I had decided that immediately after I grew up, I too would become a Provençal poet.

—For then, every year, as soon as the spring came, I would mount upon my tall, white war horse, adorned with scarlet trappings; and I would ride out to practice the Gay Science. My jongleurs would all walk behind me. I would have about twenty-five, I decided. Some of them would be playing upon lutes and gitterns and gigues and harps and trumpets, while the rest of them sang the chansons and the pastorelles and the aubades and the ballads and the sestinas which I had made up out of my own head.

All the people we met would stop and look at me.

"That is José Gasparilla himself," they would whisper.

In the trees alongside the road the birds would listen and become very jealous of my songs. They would probably dirty up my helmet just out of spite.

When we got to a castle, then I would ride impressively into the courtyard. The minute that the people who lived there heard I was José Gasparilla, the overlord of the castle and his whole family would come running, so as to help me out of my helmet and my breastplate and my hauberk and the rest of my armor. They would dress me up, instead, in a costly mantle of rare furs trimmed all around the edges with shiny gold lace and several dozen large pearls. The best-looking of the ladies of the castle would bring to me a silver basin and a fringed towel, so that I could wash my hands.

Afterward we would have a banquet, at which I would be the guest of honor. Immediately after we had finished our coffee (for my fancies were thus far anachronistic), a page would come forward. Kneeling respectfully, he would hand to me a guitar; and I would play upon it and sing about how very deeply I was in love with the most beautiful woman in the world.

Her hair was golden, her eyes were stars, and her complexion reminded you of a rosebud in June, whereas her skin was ever so much whiter than are the wind-driven snows of December, I would sing; because if you were a Provençal poet, that was the special kind of young lady you had to admire. But her heart, I would add (because this also appeared to be a rule with Provençal poets), was more hard than a millstone, so that she would not love anybody at all, not even me.

"What sort of creature can this insane woman be," everybody would say to everybody else, "that she is not heels over head in love with the handsome and celebrated Provençal poet, great José Gasparilla? And how very nicely he sings!"

The next morning we would have a tournament, at which I would unhorse all the misguided warriors who tried to oppose me. The tilting ground would be completely covered with their blood and some of their arms and legs. Their heads also would be lying around, still locked up in their helmets, because that would be the way these heads had been when I cut them off.

My jongleurs would then play upon horns and bells. After they got through, I would sing (no matter how severely I might have been wounded by my caitiff opponents) a sirvente, or a pasquinade, in which I would tell about how much I enjoyed fighting and liked to kill Saracens and other wicked people. My hearers would shout hurrah. They would clap their hands like anything; and every one of them would say:

"There is no other Provençal poet who can be compared with José Gasparilla, either at singing or in battle. He is worth ten of those Bernard de Ventadours and Pons de Capdeuils and Arnaud Daniels that his father keeps writing about. Never before to-day have we seen the like of José Gasparilla."

My father would become suitably impressed. He would stand up whenever I came into the room. And he would write another chapter, which would be the very longest chapter in his book, all about me.

21

JUST AS MY FATHER KNEW everything which had been printed in books, so did my mother know everything else. My mother was beautiful. She had brown eyes and brown hair which crinkled, but there was gold in them too. My mother was the most beautiful person in the world, as well as the most useful, because whatever you needed, you went to her and asked for it, and then she gave it to you.

It was in this way that I thought about my parents, as being all-perfect and all-powerful; and I regarded them also as being perpetual. It did not ever occur to me that my parents might become older or change at all.

82

I only would change. I would grow up, and I would be a Provençal poet—or perhaps I would be a saint. I became undecided about this. My mother was of a devout nature. She had told me a great deal about saints; and it seemed to me that the career of a saint had its special advantages.

There would be more people to admire and to talk about me as a saint than as a Provençal poet, because even the peasants, like Estevan, down in the village, knew about saints. It would be pleasant to work miracles; and then too I would have a halo. I was not certain what you did with a halo when you got ready to go to bed at night, but it probably came off without any trouble, and then you hung it up, like your hat, by the hole in it.

At all events, I assumed, tacitly, that if I did decide to be a saint, and to have my holiness and my miracle-working talked about everywhere, then my father and my mother would stay just as they were. The only difference would be that they also might have halos.

There did not seem to be any rule about this. But in pictures the mothers of some saints did have halos. Saints did not seem to have many fathers. If my mother got a halo, then after my father had told her how very becoming it was, she would not like for him to feel overshadowed by her superior state of grace. She would give it to my father at once, beyond, as people said, any shadow of doubt. I did not see, though, how a doubt could have a shadow.

Then something occurred to me that seemed curious.

"Mother," I said, "why is it that you do not have any shadow?"

"Why, but there are no shadows in any castle in Spain," said my mother, as she looked up from her sewing.

It was red and black sewing for the seat of a chair, and you did not call it sewing, but something else. I believe it was needle point.

"I thought you knew about that, José," my mother continued. "You see, people did not like to have any such gloomy things following them about everywhere. It was too depressing. So the King has made it a law that everybody should stop wearing shadows. I must have forgotten to tell you about it when we took yours away. I remember now, you were asleep at the time—and dreaming, I suppose, about being a pirate."

"It does seem curious I never missed it before," said I, consideringly. "But I can see now that my feet look a great deal better without having it wiggling around and hanging on to both of them. And what I was thinking about, anyhow, was my being a saint."

"Since when have you been canonized, my own small solemn darling?"

"Oh, but you know, mother! I mean my going to be one after I get a little bit bigger. Now St. Eulalia started at twelve. And I will be ten right after Christmas."

84

"But only yesterday, you absurd angel, you were going to be a pirate," says my mother, laughing.

"No, mother: that was day before yesterday. And pirates do not ever have halos, do they?"

"It is a question which I have never considered very closely, José; but speaking generally, I believe they do not."

"And besides that, a saint, mother, can make girls let him alone."

"Can he?" says my mother.

"I mean that he could always smite them with leprosy, or boils, or something, if they kept on following him around in the way that whining, dirty-faced little Isabel does, just like a good-for-nothing old shadow, only she is much worse, mother, she really is."

"But the Castros are our neighbors, José, and our very good friends. So I think that you ought to play with Isabel when she wants you to—at least now and then."

"But, mother, a boy does not want to play with girls!"

"I am not certain you will always think that, José," my mother informed me; "for you are a Gasparilla. And Isabel will be quite pretty when she grows up."

"But what does that matter, mother, when a girl does not have real good sense?"

My mother merely smiled. She was a considerate mother. And in this capacity she must have known—with a little sadness, I imagine—that never has any

85

mother been permitted to help her son in working out the answer to my question.

"Well, but at any rate, I think I will be a saint, after all," I decided.

22

WHEN I GOT TO BE a saint (I reflected), then my humility and my virtue would excite no less of love and admiration, everywhere upon earth, than would my intrepidity. St. José Gasparilla would go through the whole world, like St. Martin of Tours, raising up meritorious dead persons from the grave sometimes, and at other times setting fire to the temples of bad false gods and throwing down their altars and breaking up their images. That would be more fun than singing about young ladies.

And when the heathen governors and emperors had

me arrested for smashing up things in the way a saint had to do, then I would follow the fine example which had been set for me, here in our own Barcelona, by the patron saint of our neighborhood, St. Eulalia. When they began trying me, I would spit straight into the face of the presiding judge, just as she did, so as to let him see what I thought about him, and how unable he was to scare St. José Gasparilla of Montserrat.

Yes, and if the wicked tyrant got mad about my spitting in his face, and had my head cut off, why then I would pick it up; and I would walk out of his prison house with my head under my arm, like St. Denis of France, with a large flock of angels flying around me and singing; and I would get one of the angels to put it back on again.

—For a saint did not need to be afraid of anybody or anything, not even dragons. I decided to look for a dragon just as soon as I started to be a saint.

I would spur my tall, white war horse, adorned with scarlet trappings, toward the first dragon I laid eyes on; and after a prolonged and terrible combat, I would pin it to the earth with my lance, in the very best manner of St. George of Cappadocia. But when the conquered dragon got up and began to follow me around like a dog, or like Isabel de Castro, then I would not slay the broken-spirited animal, as St. George had done at Selene in Libya. That seemed to me to have been cruel, as well as wasteful.

I would keep it, instead, for a pet. A dragon would

be ever so much more impressive than a troop of jongleurs. Everybody would be quite sure to look at me when I rode by with my halo shining like a full moon, and with my tamed dragon trotting along behind me, all scaly and green-colored and breathing out clouds of fire and some smoke.

"That is St. José Gasparilla himself," people would whisper. "How very wonderful must be the virtue and the holiness of St. José Gasparilla of Montserrat, that a creature so extremely terrible should have been subdued by him!"

Then they would shout hurrah. They would clap their hands. They would take off their hats and cross themselves; they probably would kneel down; and they would start to sing hymns, which would be all about me; so that everybody everywhere would be saying:

"Never before to-day have we seen the like of St. José Gasparilla of Montserrat! There is no other saint in the Calendar who is fit to be compared with St. José Gasparilla!"

23

Meanwhile, I could not understand why such pleasant and well-behaved persons as Don Lucas de Castro and his talkative, plump little wife (who gave you sweetmeats) needed to have a girl, in the first place. A boy would have been very much more sensible, because they lived next to us, and I could have played with him, just as I played with Estevan, even though Estevan's people were nobody but villagers. So he had to do whatever I told him to do.

And besides that, if the Castros wanted a girl, it seemed to me they ought to have picked out a better one. When old Dr. Genêt brought her over to their red and white house in his gig, they should have declined to be imposed on. They ought to have returned Isabel at once.

The Castros ought to have told Dr. Genêt, quite firmly, that if this was the kind of baby he was expecting people to make out with, why, then they would send for a really good doctor from Barcelona. They might likewise, with advantage, have referred to the baby which the Gasparillas had got from him, only four years and three weeks earlier, in order to show how very noticeably his standards had deteriorated, I reflected.

For I found Isabel de Castro to be wholly repulsive.

The main trouble was that Isabel worshipped me in the most exasperating fashion. She followed after me, like a lean puppy, whenever she got the chance; and through the unfair advantage of her living next to us, she got a great many chances. Nor was I at liberty to rid myself of this persecution through pronounced violent measures, because my parents were agreed that, on account of my having all those ancestors, I ought to play with Isabel whenever she wanted me to. She had a large number of vaults and some monuments full of her own ancestors, they both said.

So I really did try to be civil to her, and to behave like a little hidalgo, sometimes. But I never found anybody to be more useless and objectionable. She was too little for you to play with satisfyingly, at any real games, such as being Sapphira when I struck her dead at my feet in the character of St. Peter, or (when I was St. Martin) to be demolished as a pagan idol, or even to figure as one of the dragon's cubs when I was St. George, with a fine, long, sharp, wooden lance which

I had made for this special game out of a clothesline prop.

Besides being too little, Isabel was skinny and knobby. Her nose turned up; and it not infrequently needed wiping. Everywhere that you could see any of her—on account of her clothes, I mean—was sprinkled with large brown freckles, except only her legs. Her legs had some thick-looking and fuzzy, pale-colored hair all over them. They reminded me, as I was at pains to inform her, of the legs of a monkey. And her arms were almost as bad.

She said the hair meant that some day she would have a great deal of money. She could keep it, I told her; and she had better be buying a scareface with some of it; for then she would not be making people sick at their stomachs with all those spots on her, like the leopard in the Bible.

After that, she began to cry. So I had to tell her, like a little hidalgo, to stop yelling, because some people thought they would come off by-and-by; and then she would be all right. Out of chivalry, I went even further in my attempt to behave like a little hidalgo; for I told her that my own mother said she was going to be quite pretty after she grew up.

Well, and then she wanted to know if I thought so? I told her not to be silly. Of course she was going to be pretty, because my mother did not tell wicked stories. My mother knew about things like that. My mother knew about everything.

"I love your mother," said Isabel, wistfully; and she added, in, I really do believe, an attempt not to hurt my feelings,—

"But I love you better, José."

You would not think a quite little girl could be so shameless. And besides that, she was holding on to my hand now.

It is in circumstances such as these that a beginning saint needs to protect his future and to be worthy of his halo. So I slapped Isabel—but not really very hard—and I told her to stop pawing at me, and to go home and get somebody to wipe her nose.

Well, and then she started back home. She almost always did what I told her to do.

And when Isabel went away it made me feel not comfortable, just somehow, to watch the hunched-up and so helpless and so small look of her shoulders. They kept shaking and shaking, pretty much as if she had hiccoughs. She was wearing some sort of girls' clothes that were made out of tiny blue and white squares, like a checkerboard, I remember.

She was so silly about everything that the little idiot was crying again. And it was not as if I had slapped her at all hard. She was just crying because I was the person who had hit her. But I did not care how much she cried. She had got exactly what she deserved for pawing at me.

Then I felt different. I did not feel like a saint any longer. I ran after her as fast as I could. I put my arms around her. I said I was sorry. I said I was going to be

92

a pirate and make lots of money for her. I said that I loved her, really and truly; and that I was going to love her always.

I was not crying, exactly, or not at least with tears, but I was sobbing so that I could not talk very well, because you ought not to hit a girl. And I do not know whether I kissed her or she kissed me. It just happened.

24

WHAT HAPPENED NEXT I do not know, either, but everything everywhere got to be so flickering and so very mixed up that Isabel was quite different. She had grown up, somehow, and so had I grown up. But I did not feel grown up. I felt light-headed, because I was talking to her about some ship or another; and I could see that my talking bothered her.

She was very much upset by whatever it was I was telling her about a ship called the *Floridablanca;* but she had become even more beautiful and more dear to me than I remembered her having been when I had first fallen in love with Isabel de Castro, forever, a great long while ago, just after Captain Sanibel had seen about my appointment at the Naval Academy.

She spoke then, saying: "I cannot but wonder at you, José; for it is not suitable that a gentleman of Spain should be going into trade. Your ancestors are no doubt astir with indignation in every one of their tombs."

I did not answer. I remembered everything now. Even in the same moment that I saw and touched her, I knew that the Isabel I loved did not exist in reality. She was a person, and the most dear of all persons, in the untroubled land without shadows, to which I had once belonged, and did not belong any more. I had strayed out of this land, in order to become a thief and a murderer.

So then, for one heartbeat, she still looked up at me, half in reproach, but all-fondly. And after that she was gone. She was gone forever; and I felt sorry about it.

"Why, but indeed it is a vast pity," someone was saying, "that we have had to hurry matters."

PART FIVE

"He loses her who gains her,
Who watches day by day
The dust of time that stains her,
The griefs that leave her gray,
The flesh that yet enchains her
Whose grace hath passed away."

25

I MUST RECORD HERE that when the ghost addressed me, I found myself to be alone with it, in a burial ground, beside a small gray chapel, partly covered with vines. This building, I discovered later, was the Shrine of Neustra Señora de la Léche y Buen Parto; and I was standing in the Cemetery of Nombre de Dios, which surrounds the chapel.

At this time, which, so nearly as I could judge, appeared to be a little while before dawn, I observed the cemetery to be a beautiful and tranquil place, in which a host of tall oleander trees preserved a perpetual twilight; yet, at the instant, this twilight was mitigated by the fact that the gaunt ghost was luminous, with a phosphorescent glowing; and so, while my dreadful companion continued speaking, I was enabled to notice that the tombs to every side of me were, for the most part, of an obviously expensive nature.

The majority of them had been builded above ground, in the form, so must I describe it, of an oblong packing case, with the coat of arms and the surprisingly numerous virtues of the tomb's occupant displayed upon the upper slab; and inasmuch as it was upon the top of a newish-looking memorial of this description that the ghost sat, and appallingly compelled my attention, I inferred that my companion must have been dead for about two or three years.

But to get on with my story without teasing your patience: I would not have my readers think that I jumped over-hastily to this conclusion; for my deduction was based upon logic. To begin with, the tomb was new; to construct a tomb of this sort requires skilled workmanship and no little time; nor, as I reflected yet further, was it customary for the bereaved relatives to give orders for the erection of a monument until after the estate of the deceased had been settled and subdivided. This, almost always, upon account of the legal formalities involved, entails somewhat more than a year's delay, before a stone mason has been selected and given the instructions upon which he acts at leisure. Here, then, were, at least, a couple of years accounted for, by logic.

To the other side, this semi-transparent and discreetly luminous gray ghost—which I observed with a deep interest, as being the first ghost that I had been privileged to encounter—seemed very slightly, if at all, older than its owner had appeared during our previous interview. I rejoiced to observe this proof that my resurrected acquaintance must have retained a full use of his faculties even until his last view of the attendant physician, because at bottom I could not help liking Don Diego de Arredondo in spite of the trick he had played upon me.

It followed that, dismissing these hasty reflections, I listened to the remarks of his ghost with a provisional friendliness.

"Yes," said Don Diego—inasmuch as thus, for convenience' sake, I shall hereinafter term that which, to be accurate, was only his ghost—"yes, it is a vast pity that we had to hurry matters. Yet the green stone is not all-powerful; nor may the dead control it. At any rate, José, you have had your jaunt into the land without shadows."

"And I was a great deal more happy there, sir, than I can hope to be in any real world," I replied, with dejection.

"Why, but yes, beyond doubt," says he; "for art tends to improve upon nature; and the art of my half-brother Antonio was of the first quality. So it has gained for you that which you desired; you have returned to the contentment of your boyhood and to the felicity of your first love. One regrets, of course, that all this should have been presented to you in a somewhat abridged version; but then, upon account of my lamented decease, in the full flower of that encyclopedia of fine qualities which I am sitting on—"

And at that, he waved one phosphorescent, long-fingered hand toward his epitaph underneath him, before he spread out both hands in a gesture of apology, so as to indicate his helplessness, as my well-wisher, after he had died and been buried.

"Nevertheless, Don Diego," I replied, "you treated candor with some parsimony when you promised to restore to me what I had lost. You did not tell me that the felicity of my first love would last but for one instant."

"Ah, but that, child, was a business transaction which involved somewhat more than 2000 pesos."

"What is your meaning, Don Diego?"

"I mean, you hulking, handsome, long-legged infant, that I had need to be rid of José Gasparilla."

"But you did not tell me that, either, sir."

"You must remember, José, that I was talking with a stranger whose honesty remained problematic. I may now tell you—my dear friend," he interpolated, with a benevolently derisive grin—"that my wife, or to be more accurate, my present widow, has stayed always somewhat in love with you. Poor Isabel is not, let us phrase it, over hasty to acquire a new idea. So, while she liked me well enough, she found me a matter of secondary interest; whereas in your picturesque iniquity she took a sort of maternal pride. I do not think that she herself knew these facts; but I did. I did not approve of these facts."

His luminous and smoke-like appearance now flick-

ered, perceptibly, with what I assumed to be a shrug;
and Don Diego said:

"I fear, child, that in those days, when I remained
subject to the frailties of the flesh, I harbored some little
jealousy. At any rate, it seemed best to get rid of you for
the rest of my life. To the other side, what with one
reason and another, I did not wish to injure Juanita's
son any more than was necessary. So I employed the
green stone in a concatenation with your self-conceit:
and the green stone has served well enough."

"It has served to send me upon a fool's errand, Don
Diego, from which I return empty-handed, after I do
not know how long a while—"

"Why, but most naturally, José, nine years count
as nine years in any and all places."

"Well, then at least, sir, now that I have to repent
humbly, I can find it a large comfort to reflect that,
during these nine years, my pirate colony, when bereft
of my shrewd and daring leadership, must have gone,
by this time, as people say, to wrack and ruin."

"But no, José, people do not say anything of the
sort, now that you repent with your own special sort of
humbleness: for you left your substitute upon earth,
and his moral principles were as shady as yours; so that
Gasparilla continues to prosper. He still intimidates all
beholders, I rejoice to inform you, at a pleasingly safe
distance from Isabel."

"Sir, you astound me—" I began.

"And for what reason?" he rejoined. "I was not ever,

I trust, overprudish; but no phantom of true refinement cares to observe his widow consorting with the shadow of a criminal."

I stayed silent. I recollected the tall young man, in the appearance of a pedlar, whom I had seen with Don Diego just after I went through the City Gates; and the singular turn of events became clear and logical. Inasmuch as I did not take with me into the land without shadows my personal shadow, it of necessity had remained in Florida; and through the abettance of dark arts such as I preferred not to consider over closely, my abandoned shadow, made vocal and endowed with the hues of vitality, had continued my abandoned career.

It followed that my late mood of repentance now figured as superfluous. I had nothing to repent for, since I was not any longer the King of Pirates; and in the wickedness of this depraved prodigy I had no further interest, beyond the desire of any other right-minded citizen to see the monster annihilated.

"I agree with you, sir," I observed, to Don Diego, "that the green stone has served us all quite well enough, now that it has secured my moral redemption without putting me to any special inconvenience. And I feel it my duty to inquire—well, but in view of your remarkable yet somewhat dubious accomplishments, sir, during your lifetime—if your present condition might not be ameliorated through a few masses?—For in that event, I am at your service, Don Diego, now that, the more thanks to your perhaps damnable or at any rate purgatorial practices, my past has become stainless and my future unclouded."

He replied gravely: "I can but thank you, José. Yet in all matters which pertain to the doctrines of our Church, my faith has stayed always unshaken. It follows that I am nowadays where I expected to be after death, and where an Arredondo is rewarded justly—nay, even ardently—for his doings upon earth."

I was about to congratulate him upon his safe entry into paradise, when at this point a cock crowed somewhere in the adjacent city of St. Augustine; and with a gracious if necessarily hasty gesture of farewell, Don Diego vanished.

26

AFTER I HAD LEFT the dusk of the cemetery, and came into open daylight—for the sun had now risen—I observed, with a lively satisfaction, that I did not cast any shadow upon the deserted roadway which was conducting me toward St. Augustine.

That at this very instant my shadow was up to some villainy or another upon the high seas, I made no doubt; and the reflection had its singular aspect: but from all points of view I found it to be gratifying. With the crimes of Gasparilla I had no more concern than with the misdeeds of Bluebeard or Iscariot or Nero, I continued to remind myself.

And indeed I gave way to a somewhat complacent consciousness of my own behavior, in comparison, not merely with the evil if accomplished King of Pirates, but with the run of mankind at large; for what other living Spanish hidalgo at forty-three (which I calculated to be my present age) could assert that throughout the last nine years he had lived without sin, in childlike innocence?

Engrossed by these edifying reflections, I passed through the City Gates, upon which I did not fail to smile with benevolence, and I so came into St. George Street. I inquired, from a barber who was making ready his tiny parlors for the day's shearing, my way to the home of Señora de Arredondo; and learned that it faced upon the Street of the Royal Hospital, near the southern end of the city.

This Carlos Genovar (for such, as I learned later, was the barber's name) directed me how to cross the Plaza, and after that to turn eastward at what his townspeople called the Artillery Lane. I obeyed his instructions; and it followed that I came to the low-walled garden in the rear of my goal before reaching its front door. And here, in this trim garden of evergreens, the dark verdure of which was as yet asparkle with dewdrops, I beheld a person upon whom my attention halted with an illimitable astonishment.

27

SHE WAS a very small person. She was skinny and knobby. Her freckles were beyond human calculation, and the morning's fresh, damp-smelling sunlight made of the hair upon her lank arms a silver-like fuzz. To be brief with my readers, she was a child of rather extraordinary ugliness; but to the glance of my astounded affection she was all-lovely.

"Isabel!" I cried out to her.

—Whereupon a raised pair of reddish-brown and unblinking eyes regarded me in alert distrust. Their

owner did not know who I was, she declared with decision; and so, how could I know who she was? And
besides that, her mama did not like to have strange
gentlemen in their garden.

The imp spoke to no purpose, for I was already in
it. And I touched this child with a sort of reverence. I
became indeed somewhat light-headed: for I was now
thinking that I did love the brat, really and truly, just
as I had promised to do; and that I was going to love her
always, even after she had grown up to be middle-
aged and fat and garrulous and all-overbearingly self-
complacent.

"To your mama, Isabel," I assured her, "I am not
wholly a stranger, nor to you either. It is true that our
last meeting occurred in circumstances upon which I
may not dwell with wisdom. I was then very rude to
you. And for that reason—like a little hidalgo—I have
come back, from out of another world, to make my
amends. The entire affair, you perceive, is quite simple
when once it is weighed rationally."

That I must be sort of crazy was young Isabel's instant deduction; I did not belong in their garden; and
anyhow, who was I, to be coming through their side
gate when nobody was more than about half-awake?

Now that for the first time I considered this matter,
here was a question which startled me. Inasmuch as my
truant shadow had decamped, not merely with my
professional practice and my business equipments, but
with my Christian name and my surname also, I ap-

peared to have become anonymous; and in spheres where nobody else remained nameless, any such eccentricity upon my part, I reflected, might be attended by inconvenience.

For the while, though, my unprecedented problem was deferred by a woman's voice. It stated, with a condescension which was not unfriendly:

"If you had any sense whatever, José Gasparilla, you would not be coming here at the risk of your life, no, not for one solitary instant, and especially before breakfast, with the police offering a reward for your capture signed by the Governor himself, Enrique White in large letters, and a picture that is no more like you than if you were another Irishman—"

I looked up, from the child, toward my adored Isabel. I did not speak. And Isabel stopped scolding me. We merely looked at each other for a moment. Then I put my arm about the plump, squat-figured widow of Don Diego de Arredondo, and I kissed her.

"And now, please, do you tell me just how many stepchildren I am going to have?" I requested, so as to preserve a well-bred demeanor of levity.

My voice broke, though, in a manner which I found distressingly bucolic. I said then,—

"I have come home, Isabel."

She answered: "And it is quite time that you did, if you ask me, after sixteen years and three months of behaving in the way that you have behaved; nor is there any least need for you to be arguing about it. We can make out with eggs and bacon, I suppose, this morning. It is absolutely everything we have in the house. And poor Diego's delight in our having a girl at last was simply beyond any human description. So there are six of them; and it is only about the police I am worried—"

Her voice changed. Her hand touched my hand now that Isabel said,—

"Oh, my own dear José!"

And the prosaic housewife, as I observed with emotion, was weeping a little; nor can I swear that my own eyes were entirely arid. In brief, there was never a middle-aged couple who behaved more absurdly before breakfast, in the presence of an unapproving small person. She remarked, with detachment, that both of us must just certainly be as crazy as Junebugs; and that, for her part, she wanted something to eat.

"And so do I," I assured one Isabel, in the same instant that I told the other,—

"My character is now as far above reproach as is my happiness beyond description."

I added that I would explain everything after breakfast.

28

It surprised and soothed me alike to note with how large calmness my adored Isabel received an account of happenings which still seem to me to have been improbable.

—For her verdict ran to the effect that, inasmuch as the new Governor of East Florida was an Irishman, who told some quite amusing stories, we did not have to bother about that, because he had never laid eyes on me, and neither had anybody else, so far as she knew, in St. Augustine, apart from my being a good nine years older now and not a bit more like my picture upon those broadsides than the Queen of Sheba.

"Yes, but—" I said.

The main point (Isabel continued) was that so long as another José Gasparilla went on calling himself the King of Pirates and behaving outrageously, because there was simply not any other word for it, with his headquarters upon the Gulf of Mexico, no person who lived in St. Augustine every day could be mistaken for

111

him, even if they did have the same name; and it was quite a pleasant city with an excellent school for the boys. The mosquitoes, you could not deny, were annoying during the summer months. And when little Isabel got older, there was the convent school, too.

"Nevertheless—" I began.

Any number of people had the same name (Isabel resumed), and especially here in St. Augustine, where almost everybody was somebody else's cousin, or perhaps an uncle; nor was a shadow of any possible use to anybody, except only, when you came to think over the matter sensibly, exactly what Diego had done with it. Some people might call it magic, or even sorcery, which no Christian person would ever dream of defending, or at least not as a general rule; but since we did not have to tell anybody about it, and when it had worked out so as to help every one of us, because it was really a great comfort to know that Diego was already in paradise, why, then you might far better call it a miracle.

"Still—" I replied.

Miracles were entirely respectable, Isabel pointed out. And in fact, if it had been sorcery, he would now be in purgatory at the very least. So what, after all, was there for me to keep on arguing about, without listening to what she was trying to tell me for my own good? It was so exactly like a man, and you could not help wondering at them. Why, but I had every right in the world to keep my own name here in St. Augustine, with all those broadsides to prove that I looked like somebody else—or at any rate, that I did not look in the least bit like him—if only because I had it first. And for thirty-four years longer, she added with decision.

In this manner did my future wife dispose of my nominal difficulties; and in the event, I found out she was speaking with wisdom.

I may add here that she continued to be in the right about everything after we had been married. She admitted it herself. And while I did not always understand, not instantly, just what my adored Isabel was talking about, yet I soon learned that, beneath the unexpected sorties and the parentheses and the leisurely back-eddies of her monologues, a well-balanced mind was going about the day's work serenely.

So I respected her judgment in all matters; I deferred to her decisions; and for this reason (now that the relationships of our childhood had been so far reversed that it was I who did what she told me to do) we lived together without any wrangling. And I was troubled only by a few random apprehensions lest, in some fashion, my released shadow might be emphasizing its complete independence of me.

Nor during this calm period did we lack for whatever money we might require. I unearthed, at my convenience, four of the treasure hoards which the King of Pirates had buried, and his ill-gotten gains were directed by me to philanthropic and pious ends. His villainy supported our household; it educated my stepchildren; it dressed my dear wife as finely as she elected; and it donated, with a liberal hand, alike to the indigent and the infirm, as well as to the religious activities of our parish and of the Diocese of Louisiana and the Floridas in general.

That I failed to dig up more than a modest portion of this other Gasparilla's opulence is attributable to the circumstance that in St. Augustine the expenses of living in comfort were moderate. We had not any need of more money than we already possessed, the more thanks to his depravity. And inasmuch as the King of Pirates' abominable doings did not otherwise affect my contented and prosperous home circle, there was no reason at all for me to be thinking about him, so I tried to believe.

Meanwhile, I did not pretend to hide my relationship with this other José Gasparilla. I instead talked about it, to the leading citizens of St. Augustine, with a premeditated tediousness. That we sprang from the same family, and that until he began to live improperly, we were attached to each other, I admitted with candor. The woodcut upon those repellant broadsides which offered a reward for my capture I declared to be an excellent likeness of him. I furthermore took pains to invent a number of extremely dull anecdotes concerning my famous kinsman, which I prefaced with a beaming, "Now I am certain it will amuse you to hear this." I told them over and over again to my bored auditors.

And it followed that, when in place of concealing, I

advertised after this fashion, my former connection with the King of Pirates, people listened to me with the indifference which is ordinarily accorded to the reminiscences of a garrulous old gentleman who is past the prime of his faculties.

In this way did I become exceedingly well-thought-of by the genteel; and I lived secure against any earthly mischance—or so at least I assured myself—except only the not impossible malevolence of my wicked shadow. After having been compelled to dance attendance upon me throughout some thirty-four years, this notoriously proud creature might have come to regard me with a particular disfavor, I reflected, without any at all marked sentiments of elation.

29

So THEN, while in the city of St. Augustine I lived with a respectability which uneasiness flavored, my shadow continued to thrive in the Gulf of Mexico and upon the Spanish Main as a buccaneer without any parallel; his vigor and his ruthlessness remained topics which I discussed painstakingly, with a befitting amount of moral indignation; and upon almost every clear afternoon I agreed with the other sedate loiterers of my own age and social condition who had forgathered upon the green benches of the Plaza, for checkers' and dominoes' and gossip's sake, that something really ought to be done about it. The rascal needed to be put in his proper place, I remarked severely.

And yet, so far as went my not having him at my heels, nobody criticized this omission; nor, I believe, did any person ever notice that I had no shadow. It was a shortcoming which injured no one; and in fact, my sole worry, nowadays, was lest my estranged companion might be returning to annoy its creator.

Then at long last, while we Spanish and Minorcan gentlemen deplored at leisure the regrettable behavior of the King of Pirates, the United States of America decided that he had become intolerable. Mr. Monroe spoke with decision; and Mr. Smith Thompson took action.

It thus followed that a special squadron of six vessels, so we heard in the Plaza (from a gentleman then resident in Louisiana, whose name escapes me) had been dispatched against my runagate shadow, including one sloop of war, the *Hornet*, and two brigs, the *Spark* and the *Enterprise*, as well as three schooners, the *Grampus*, the *Shark*, and the *Porpoise*. And we heard likewise how this miniature navy, an exact week before my sixty-fifth birthday, had tracked down and surrounded Gasparilla's sloop, near his five islands, compelling him to retire landward into the body of water which is now called Charlotte Harbor.

When thus confronted with capture, and after having defended his vessel with an intrepidity worthy of a more elevated cause, the King of Pirates gave vent to an oration in which the expressed sentiments were of a nature far less praiseworthy, by the judicious, than was his diction to the more highly trained taste of cognoscenti. He then wrapped a length of anchor chain about his waist and shoulders, and with a final objurgation, such as decorum prompts me to omit from these pages, he plunged overboard.

All but a dozen of his misled followers were killed in the battle preceding Gasparilla's exit from infamy; and eleven of these had been hanged, in the city of New Orleans, without delay. Of the King of Pirates' crew, a cabin boy alone, who upon account of his tender age and repentant expressions had been sentenced to ten years imprisonment, survived at this instant, in a dungeon at Baton Rouge. And the body of my shadow—so we were yet furthermore informed by the gentleman from Louisiana, whose red side-whiskers remain more firmly imprinted in my memory than does, by ill luck, his name—had not ever been recovered.

Such then was the news which came to us in the

Plaza, where the gentry of St. Augustine were accustomed to assemble upon clear afternoons. Do you let me assure you that after having heard this tragic story, I at once glanced downward. And that which I found at my feet did not surprise me, inasmuch as, for the sake of coolness, we were then sitting in the shade of a half-dozen fine, large live oaks. I was thus forced to defer finding out, at some opportunity more propitious, whether or not my shadow had resumed its normal and harmless functions.

—For there, after all, was no particular need for any hurry about the settling of this question. To me, in my unassailable respectability, it now did not matter. The King of Pirates had been removed from the arena of his indiscretions by that far-seeing Providence which in the long run defends the reputable, I decided humbly, with a warm glow of gratitude.

30

Since a quiet walk promotes digestion, I now and then stroll toward the City Gates, with the aid of my predecessor's ebony cane; I stand leaning upon it very much as he did when I last saw him in flesh and blood; and I regard pensively the palm-shadowed road which extends before me.

It leads, I reflect, to the cemetery alone, nowadays. Nor may I at all reasonably hope to regain the incurious happiness and the sense of complete protection and the high-flown fancies of childhood, so long as the key to these matters remains to the right-hand side of an upper drawer to a tall mahogany bureau, along with my small socks, in the land without shadows.

Yet furthermore: I am not certain that, even if I had the power to do so, I would care to re-enter the land without shadows through irregular channels such as smack of heresy and of a rebellion against every adult person's normal bankruptcy as to complete happiness. It appears wiser for a respected citizen, at my time of life, to proceed uncomplainingly along the road which conducts you toward the Cemetery of Nombre de Dios; and so to obtain, in a paradise that is properly authorised, the rewards for his sober conduct and for his piety upon the inner side of the City Gates.

I do not fail, I believe, to exhibit both qualities, nowadays, inasmuch as late middle life has removed from me any special temptation to act otherwise.

Behold me then, after so many misadventures, and it may be some human errors, thus safely and thus snugly established as a reputable, rather smug bulwark of the True Faith, with a neat bank balance. In this rôle I am respected by everybody in St. Augustine, as well as by a number of the better-thought-of persons in Jacksonville and in Tallahassee also. My stepchildren (except only Lucas, who died at seventeen, of the yellow fever) have developed into estimable citizens, and have married befittingly. They now have children of their own, who call me grandfather.

To the companionship of the one woman whom I have loved, with an heroic and singular affection, I have become so far habituated that I would not like to have her changed in any respect. She pampers me; she spares no labor to further my physical comfort; she now and then addresses me as Diego; nor at any time does she omit to express her complete disapproval of whatever I may have done without consulting her in advance, or may suggest doing. I know that, at heart, my adored

Isabel looks upon me as being the least gifted of her children.

In brief, we have here an authentic romance in which, after some scufflings with evil, the hero becomes a husband and lives happily ever afterward, I reflect; for even though I have not been made exactly happy, yet I remain well enough satisfied, by the moral and financial regeneration of José Gasparilla.

EXPLICIT